PLAY NIMRO[

Christopher and Nick hav[
sive friendship that isolates them from the crowd.
Nick seems to have all the ingredients for popularity – looks, talent, background – but remains
indifferent to it, aloof and self-contained. It is
Christopher, awkward and sensitive, who is much
more acutely aware of their outsider status.
Together they occupy an inner world: writing,
listening to music, and role-playing as Guy and
Oliver. Through Guy and Oliver they communicate their most secret thoughts, ideas and dreams
for the future.

Then Sal appears on the scene. Lively, popular
and mischievously teasing she tempts Christopher
away from this private world with Nick. The
resulting tensions, rifts and painful insights crowd
in upon all three – and for Nick they reach crisis
point.

Powerful and moving, but with a great sense of
verve and wit, the story of Christopher and Nick
unfolds compellingly towards its climax.

Jean Ure always knew she was going to be a writer
and had her first book published while she was
still at school. She left school at 17 to be a writer,
but found it hard to make a living and tried many
jobs: nursing, typing, washing-up and working for
NATO and UNESCO in Paris before going to
Drama School and pursuing a career in the
theatre.

Now a full-time writer, she lives in London with
her husband, an actor whom she met at drama
school, four dogs and two cats.

04162

ALSO BY JEAN URE

PLAY NIMROD
FOR HIM

Jean Ure

THE BODLEY HEAD
LONDON

British Library Cataloguing in Publication Data
Ure, Jean
  Play Nimrod for him.
  I. Title
  823'.914 [J]

  ISBN 0–370–31184–1

First published in 1990 by The Bodley Head Children's Books
An imprint of the Random Century Group Ltd
20 Vauxhall Bridge Road, London, SW1V 2SA

Random Century Australia (Pty) Ltd
89-91 Albion Street, Surry Hills, NSW 2010, Australia

Random Century New Zealand Ltd
PO Box 40-086, Glenfield, Auckland 10, New Zealand

Century Hutchinson South Africa (Pty) Ltd
PO Box 337, Bergvlei, 2012, South Africa

Typeset by Falcon Graphic Art Ltd
Wallington, Surrey
Printed in Great Britain by Cox and Wyman Ltd

To Ann-Janine Murtagh,
who came to know this book even better
than its author

I

In the narrow guest-house bed, in the same scabby, shabby, totally featureless guest-house bedroom as he had had last year, and the year before, and the year before that, with a pillow lumped over his face to shut out all contact with the mid-morning sun, pulsating on the other side of the porridge-textured curtains, Christopher lay on his back enjoying forbidden fruits. *Stop that, sailor! You'll go blind! Ruin your constitution, lad! Reduce yourself to a state of drivelling imbecility* (if the heavy metals in the water supply didn't get to him first).

The thing was, he was anxious it should be known, even if only within the confines of his own consciousness, he never set out with the deliberate intent of abusing himself. It was more subversive than that. What happened was that he would start off in all innocence on a perfectly harmless thought about Guy and Oliver, and by degrees, almost without him being aware of it, it would degenerate into what could only be described as an orgy.

He never meant it to. He swore he never meant it to. Well, perhaps he *half* meant it to, but for all that, the game was not without its rules. There was too much of the would-be writer in him to permit just anything to happen. The basic rule was that fantasy or no, the thing had to hang together.

Like, for example, his current story line, which was Oliver seeing Guy off at Heathrow and being hijacked in the Jag on the way back to their flat. That was plausible. The hijackers were obviously aware of Oliver's identity. They obviously knew that he was an up-and-coming writer – 'Young Novelist of Promise' – and that his parents were Dr Malcolm Hamilton, Professor of English at Cambridge University, and Jane Hunter Hamilton, RA, the well-known portrait painter. They were obviously going to hold him to ransom. That was OK. It was the next bit that worried him; the bit where they took him back to their hideout and suddenly revealed themselves as women in drag. He wasn't too sure about the gang-bang which followed. He kept meaning to moderate it.

This morning, he left it too late: the gang-bang rushed upon him before he could stop it. He had just reached the point of no return when the door crashed open and his mother came thumping in. The result, needless to say, was disastrous.

'*Christopher!*' Bang-thud-stamp across the carpet. Louise could never walk anywhere quietly. 'Do you know what the time is? It's gone half-past ten! I seriously begin to wonder –' he clutched, defensively, at the sheet – 'whether you have sleeping sickness. How you can come away on holiday and spend all your time lying in bed with your eyes shut –' *Rip*. That was the curtains. She always hauled at them as if she had some kind of personal grudge against them – 'I simply cannot understand.'

2

From under his pillow, he said: 'I wasn't asleep, I was thinking.'

'So why can't you get up and think? And what are you doing with a pillow over your face?' She snatched at it. He winced, as the sunlight hit him. 'What are you *doing*?' said Louise.

'Trying to suffocate myself.'

'Well, stop it!' She stood, holding the pillow to her chest, looking down with her usual air of exasperation. *I don't know, Christopher! What am I to do with you?* 'Gran and I are off now, we're going down to the Front. Are you going to get up at all, or –'

'Yes, all right. I'll get up.' He held on fiercely to the sheet, in case she should attempt to drag it off him. Once, at home, in the middle of winter, she had taken his duvet away and hung it over the banisters. He had been forced to get up whether he liked it or not. He didn't *think* she would try that trick now, he thought it would probably embarrass her as much as it would him, seeing him naked, but he wasn't taking any chances. 'I'll get dressed in just a few minutes. I'll come and join you.'

'You don't necessarily have to join us,' said Louise, 'but at least make sure you get out of that bed. It's not healthy, stuffing indoors on a day like this. And what are you going to do about breakfast?'

'I'll find something.'

'We pay for your breakfast, you know. Whether you have it or not. It's just a sheer waste.' Louise dropped the pillow back on to the bed and trod heavily across to the door. 'It's just a waste bringing you on holiday at all.'

He might have retorted, so why do it?, but she had already gone. He heard her footsteps clumping down the stairs to the entrance hall, where his grandmother would be waiting, tutting and muttering. *It's not natural, a boy of his age. It's just not natural . . .*

He hadn't wanted to come on holiday with them. He'd begged and pleaded to be allowed to go to Switzerland with Nick to stay with Nick's grandmother, but his mother wouldn't hear of it.

'We can't afford it,' she'd said; and when he'd pointed out that they wouldn't have to afford it because Nick's grandmother had offered to pay for him: 'I'm not accepting charity from Nick's grandmother.'

She wouldn't even let him stay at home in Holt Wood by himself. 'A boy of your age? – You're only sixteen, you know.' So what nameless and appalling acts did she think a sixteen-year-old was going to be guilty of, left on his own for two weeks? She could hardly be scared of wild parties. The one thing they were always on at him about was that he never *went* to parties – 'You never mix with people, you never go anywhere . . . it's not natural!'

He threw off the sheet (carefully examining it for stains), slung his dressing-gown round himself and shuffled off to the communal bathroom at the far end of the corridor. On his way he passed a window which looked out on to what last year had still been the front garden, but this year had been cemented over to form a mini car park for the convenience of those guests who had cars. (Louise didn't: couldn't afford it. Couldn't drive, come to that.)

He saw them both, Louise and his grandmother, cross the road and set off towards the Front. His grandmother was done up like a parcel in a thick tweedy coat with her hair in a pink hair net. Louise was in her beach outfit, stout flat shoes and plastic mac. She was carrying her

4

old straw beach-basket, full of rugs and packed lunches and polythene bags containing long strips of knitting, plus the two folding chairs which they had brought with them from home. You could hire chairs by the day, or even by the week, but as she said, why pay out what little money one had on objects one could just as easily – well, almost as easily – provide for oneself? He supposed she was right. He supposed, also, that if he were a gallant and dutiful son, instead of a slothful, self-abusing, anti-social slug-a-bed, he would be down there right now, carrying the wretched things for her.

As she reached the corner, Louise half-turned and looked back. Hastily he shrank away, moving on down the passage before she could catch sight of him.

Louise, his mother: his mother, Louise. He must get into the habit. The trouble was, he still didn't *think* of her as Louise; he thought of her as 'my mother'. 'My mother' defined her – it defined the role she played in his life. 'Louise' bestowed upon her the validity of being an individual in her own right, totally divorced and separate from himself; he hadn't yet learnt to cope with that concept. Still, he'd only been doing it a couple of months. Nick had been calling his mother Susan for the last couple of years, though it was easier for Nick since Susan Sheringham was undeniably an individual in her own right, totally and utterly removed from Nick, so much so that there were times they seemed in no way even remotely connected.

When Christopher had announced to Louise that he was going to call her by her name – 'It's ridiculous calling people by the roles they play ... you don't call people "Plumber" or "Neighbour" ' – Louise had accepted it with surprisingly good grace. He had thought she would protest, but all she had said was, 'If it makes

5

you feel more grown up.' (Clever, that: cutting him down to size. She did these things purely by instinct, not even knowing it.) It had been his grandmother who had done all the protesting: 'Disrespectful, that's what I call it!'

Louise, mildly, had said that it was 'The modern way . . . they even call some of their teachers by their Christian names these days.'

'Well, they shouldn't! It shouldn't be allowed. A teacher is a person in authority.' And then she had sniffed, that puritanical, self-righteous sniff of hers, and said: 'You needn't think you're going to go round calling me Eleanor.'

He had no desire to go round calling his grandmother Eleanor. He had no desire to go round calling her anything at all, unless perhaps it was a wittering old windbag. And why not? If she could go round telling everyone she met, even, very often, total strangers, that he was unnatural – 'Unnatural, that boy is. Head stuck in a book, never gets out, never does anything' – well, he really didn't see why he should be expected to hold back. He only did so for his mother's sake. 'It upsets me,' she said, 'when you and your gran fall out. We all have to live together,' she said. And, 'It is your grandmother's house,' she said. 'If it hadn't been for her –'

Oh, horror heaped on horror! They might have ended up in a *council house*.

'You wouldn't like it,' said Louise, 'so don't pretend you would.'

Could a council house be worse than a 1930s semi with 'through lounge' and 'serving hatch' and coloured glass sunrise (or was it sunset?) blazing across the front door? He thought of the sprawling estates – Longshaw, Brabourne, Tipsy Hill – and he knew that yes, it could.

It didn't make it any easier, having to bite his tongue.

It was eleven o'clock when he finally emerged from the guest-house into the light of day. He had a headache from too much sleep and it was almost a relief to be out in the street, although there was nothing to do once he was there. Smeaton-on-Sea was strictly for wrinklies.

'I suppose you'd like everything to be swinging!' his grandmother had said. She'd only said it because swinging was her latest buzz word. (She'd picked it up from a television programme about the Sixties.) In the next breath she accused him of being 'All hoity-toity and highbrow . . . thinks himself far too clever for the rest of us.' She couldn't have it both ways; she couldn't have him hankering after pop culture *and* being an intellectual snob – another of her favourite epithets. 'Quite the little intellectual snob, aren't we?'

The plain fact was, she disapproved whatever he did.

He decided to live up to his image and buy some improving literature to read on the beach. In his last letter, Nick had mentioned that he was reading Sartre – *La Nausée*, from which he had quoted liberally. In French, needless to say. Nick, of course, had an unfair advantage. He had spent every summer since he was nine years old wandering the Continent with his wonderful rackety grandmother. Christopher, for all he had a flair for languages, couldn't really hope to compete. Still, that was no reason for not at least making the attempt.

There was only one bookshop in Smeaton: it had no copy of *La Nausée* in French, English or any other tongue. The woman who ran it said she was so sorry, but they just didn't have any call for books in foreign languages; not in Smeaton. He could see that they wouldn't. People didn't come here to tax their brains, they came here (mainly) to retire and then to die. He thanked her politely, not holding it against her, and she said there was a second-hand shop just up the road, why didn't he try there?

The second-hand shop dealt mostly with junk; but in a cardboard carton of books, tucked away between a Jeffrey Archer and *The Story of O*, he came across an aged copy of *Utopia* for 10p. He decided to make do with that. It wasn't in the original Latin, but it could definitely be classed as Improving Literature, and anyway, not even Nick could manage to stagger through it in Latin. Nick might be an academic whizz, but he wasn't your actual boy genius.

He bought a cup of coffee and a Cornish pasty as a replacement for breakfast and wandered munching along the Front in search of Louise and his grandmother. He found them sitting on their folding chairs in the teeth of a hectoring gale. This was the south coast, and there almost always was a hectoring gale, but it took only an hour and twenty minutes to get there by train from Holt Wood and was thus to be recommended. Furthermore, it was familiar. She couldn't understand it, his grandmother always said, folks spending time and money going off on these long journeys to foreign parts when they could get the same thing far better and cheaper at home. (What she was really knocking was Nick going off to the Continent every year. His grandmother didn't like Nick – 'Too hoity-toity by half,' she said.)

'Ah, so you've got here,' said Louise.

She was knitting, placidly, seemingly impervious to the gale. His grandmother was reading the *Daily Mail*, folded into a minute square so that it wouldn't be buffeted. Christopher sat down on the stones, turned up his jacket against the wind and half-heartedly opened

Utopia. He no longer felt any inclination to read Improving Literature. He wished now that he'd bought *The Story of O*, instead. It had had a naked woman on the front and would have upset his grandmother.

The problem with Improving Literature was that it needed concentration. Smeaton beach, in the teeth of a hurricane, was not the place, especially with the added accompaniment of his grandmother, alternately sniffing and sucking on her false teeth. Every now and again she would relay snippets of so-called news to Louise – ' "Social Security Swindler Sizzles in Sunshine", "Unmarried Mothers given Preferential Treatment", "Christian Ethics Sacrificed in Name of Liberalism" ' – and Louise would shake her head and rustle more wool from out of its plastic bag and go click-click-click with her plastic knitting needles.

He could hardly ask them to shut up, just because he'd chosen to conduct an intellectual wrestling match with Thomas More. Even he realized that. It was their patch of beach, they had got here first. They had every right to sit and suck their teeth and rustle.

Idly he scooped up a handful of pebbles. He wondered if he could tell Nick that he had met a man in a second-hand bookshop – an *antiquarian* bookshop – who had been an intimate friend of Jean-Paul Sartre.

'French, of course –' He began lobbing his pebbles, one by one, into a nearby rock pool. 'Michel, his name was. Michel –' he paused, as he sought for a likely-sounding surname – 'Michel Lautrec.' Lob, splash. 'He gave me a cup of coffee – gave me a *Pernod* –' Lob – 'and we sat there chatting –' Damn! – 'for about – oh! Most of the morning. *En Français, bien sûr. Il m'a dit –*'

'Do you mind?' said Louise. She bent, fretfully, and

rubbed at her ankle. 'What's the matter with you? Can't you just sit still for a change? Anyone would think you'd got St Vitus' Dance.'

First it was sleeping sickness, then St Vitus' Dance. She ought to make up her mind.

'I'm cold.' He began to construct a cairn of stones over his feet. Louise, pointedly, removed her legs from the firing line. 'It's fatuous, coming away for seaside holidays in this sort of climate.'

'Oh, you think everything's fatuous!'

'No, I don't. Only those things which obviously are.'

'Just tell me something that obviously isn't ... honestly! I've never known anyone so perpetually discontented.'

'That's the modern generation for you,' urged his grandmother. She was always spoiling for a fight. 'Too used to having everything at the flick of a switch ... electronic this, electronic that. Take away all their clever gadgets and what are they left with? Nothing! No inner resources, that's their trouble.'

Loftily, he turned back to Thomas More. For form's sake he ploughed through another seven pages, but the words were just words, without form or meaning. He scooped up another handful of pebbles and began composing a conversation between himself and Michel Lautrec.

'*Il m'a dit qu'il y avait une fois –*'

Not that Nick was likely to believe him. Christopher had described Smeaton too often and in too much scathing detail for him to swallow tales of people who had been intimate with anyone even remotely worth being intimate with. Nick was the one who met all the fascinating people; all the sophisticated, cultured people who played in orchestras or wrote poetry and knew what went on behind the scenes in the artistic world that he and Christopher were going to enter, in a blaze of glory, after their joint careers at Oxford or Cambridge. He would just laugh if Christopher tried it on.

Moodily, he flung another pebble.

'There he goes again,' said his grandmother.

'Christopher, do you have to?' Louise said it wearily. It wasn't so much a protest as a meaningless mechanical utterance, indicative of resignation, or perhaps despair. He was well aware that his mother had long since given up on him. Unguardedly, without thinking, he said: 'I'm starving! When are we going to have something to eat?'

His grandmother smiled malevolently over her folded square of newspaper. 'If some of us got up earlier in the mornings,' she said, 'we could eat our breakfast along with everyone else.'

'Where's the point of getting up in this lousy place?' He turned on her, angry at having been caught in a trap of his own making. He always swore he would remain aloof and unmoved by his grandmother's taunts, but when it came to it he never failed to be tempted by them. 'Might just as well be dead.'

His grandmother set down her newspaper, alert and eager. She leaned towards him. 'That's a fine attitude, I must say, for someone of your age . . . if you feel like that, I wonder you think it worth while to go on living at all.'

'*Croyez-vous que la vie vaille la peine d'être vécue jusqu'à la fin?*' he muttered. His grandmother, delighted – she was never happier than when scrapping with him – clicked her false teeth.

'Showing off again with our clever foreign languages . . . what's that supposed to mean when it's at home?'

11

He did his best to sound as weary as Louise: 'Does one really believe that life is worth living right to the very end?'

'So why not say it in English?'

'Because it wasn't written in English.'

His grandmother sniffed. 'I should say it was a piece of rudeness to talk in a foreign language when people don't know what you're saying – especially when it's thanks to those people you've had the opportunity to learn it in the first place. A bit of gratitude wouldn't come amiss, instead of all this grumbling and groaning. I sometimes think you don't realize the sacrifices your mother has had to make to send you to that posh school you go to.'

She hadn't had to make any sacrifices. He'd got a scholarship to Astley, his mother didn't have to contribute so much as a penny piece.

'At your age,' said his grandmother, 'I was out earning my own living. I daresay we both of us were . . . isn't that right, Lou? Weren't you out earning your living?' Louise nodded but said nothing, engaged in counting stitches. 'Might do someone else I know a bit of good to get off his bottom and start shifting for a change. Other boys have to. I remember your father, when he was just a tiny lad, going out delivering his newspapers . . . used to get up before school, six o'clock every morning, winter and summer, never missed a day. Did it for years, just to earn himself a bit of extra pocket money.'

Yes, and had ended up ripping off his best mate that he had gone into business with. Before Christopher had attained the age of consciousness, that had been. They had done their best to keep it from him, but he had read about it, subsequently, in a newspaper report secreted by Louise at the back of her underwear drawer. There had been a death certificate in there, too. Carcinomatosis, it had said; whatever that was.

His grandmother still tried to pretend that none of it had ever happened. He might have reminded her of it had he been feeling really evil: once again, he bit his tongue. There would only be recriminations. Although unsatisfactory in almost every conceivable respect, his father had nonetheless been his grandmother's sole off-spring and thus continued to be cherished in spite of his failings. Only once, in a moment of ungovernable rage, goaded beyond endurance by his grandmother's constant taunts of unnaturalness, had Christopher given way to spite and screamed at her, what would she expect from someone who had had a rip-off merchant for a father? His mother had slapped him and burst into tears. His grandmother, he knew, had never forgiven him.

Louise, fearful perhaps of a repeat, suddenly came to a decision. She laid down her knitting. 'We'll have an early lunch,' she said.

'That's right,' said his grandmother. 'Pander to him.'

At two o'clock they were due to go on a coach trip to a nearby village to gaze on Lord Somebody-or-other's ancestral home and gardens. Christopher, who disapproved on principle of lords and wouldn't have been caught dead gazing at anybody's ancestral home had only agreed to go for want of anything better to do. He left Louise and his grandmother at the entrance to the grounds and said he would meet them later.

'Suit yourself,' said his grandmother.

There was a church in the village. Churches as such held no particular interest for him, but he thought he might just as well go in and have a look. There was a board outside advertising times of mass, which presumably meant it was Catholic. Sceptical though he mostly was of the claims of religion, the Catholic faith, with all its paraphernalia of rosaries and crucifixes, its strange arcane rituals, its celibate priesthood, held a secret fascination for him. He occasionally envied those such as Nick, who, having been brought up in it since birth, were able to treat it with such cool, cavalier indifference.

He had been into churches with Nick and stood silently watching as quite unself-consciously Nick set about the prescribed rituals, doing those things that Catholics did, dipping his finger in the holy water, crossing himself, genuflecting. It had always faintly embarrassed Christopher; he had never quite succeeded in working out why. He thought perhaps it was the very fact that it was Nick – Nick, his friend and intellectual equal, unashamedly, in public, performing acts so nakedly, almost indecently primitive. Not to follow suit was to mark oneself indelibly as a mere day-tripper, no better than the coach party gone off to ogle Lord So-and-so's mansion; still he couldn't bring himself to do it. Unlike Nick he was too self-conscious, too scared lest a real Catholic should be watching and catch him out in some fundamental error which betrayed him.

He hung around the central aisle, titillating himself with the thought of bending his knee and making the sign of the cross, still not quite daring, until in the end a real Catholic did appear, in the shape of a priest wearing a dog collar, at which he instantly took fright and slunk back out into the churchyard to look at the graves.

The graves, in fact, were interesting, some of them dating back as far as the eighteenth century, but he didn't pay them as much attention as he might have done. A thought was occurring to him. Slowly, bit by bit, as he wandered amongst the tombstones, it began to take shape. He sank down on to his haunches, his back against a yew tree, trying to develop it, to work out the details, so that he could present it to Nick as a *fait accompli* on his return from holiday.

A thought, by definition, was a thought about Guy and Oliver. He couldn't remember now the precise moment when Guy and Oliver had entered their lives. He had an idea it had been something to do with an English project, dating from their second form days. They had been teamed off in pairs, alphabetically, and because that had been the term when Derek Siegenberg had had to stay in hospital with his spine in a plaster cast, Seymour and Sheringham had been shunted together.

The project had been to do with writing books. They had all had to make up a story and type it out on the word processor and then make it into book form. If Guy and Oliver hadn't figured in that first literary attempt, they had certainly come into being very shortly after, for he clearly remembered sitting on the edge of the Field with Nick, one summer breaktime, writing out a chapter heading, 'In Which Our Heroes Meet', in an exercise book filched from the form stationery cupboard. The heroes could only have been Guy and Oliver.

Since that time they had all four of them, Nick and Christopher, Guy and Oliver, grown up together (albeit with a seven-year age gap) until the make-believe of 'Our Heroes' had become almost more real than reality.

Oliver was Christopher's character, and somewhere inside himself Christopher was vaguely and reluctantly aware that Oliver represented what he would like to be. Oliver was six feet tall, with straight fair hair, brown eyes and a clear skin. Christopher, by contrast, was on the short side, and sturdy: he had black hair, coarse and displeasingly (in his view) kinked, his eyes were ordinary blue-green, his nose freckled, and somewhat stub. Oliver, though sensitive, was nonetheless sure of himself: Christopher, oversensitive to the point of paranoia, was sure neither of himself nor of anyone else.

He wondered, occasionally, whether Guy represented what Nick would like to be – or whether in fact Guy *was* Nick. Whether there were two Nicks. The Nick of every day, clever, contained, above-it-all, seemingly so secure in his own destiny – as indeed how should he not be? Nick had everything going for him. Looks, talent, background. He never had to struggle, as ordinary beings did. Nature had showered him with gifts in abundance; had endowed him, had he only chosen to make use of them, with all the right ingredients for popularity. Nick did not choose, and therein lay the puzzle – and also, perhaps, much of the fascination.

For Christopher, craving so desperately the good opinion of the world, Nick's apparently quite genuine indifference was at one and the same time both enviable and totally beyond the realms of his own comprehension. He sometimes thought that to be thus immune from the petty paltriness of others was possible only for the favoured few: secure in his own brilliance, Nick could afford to give two fingers to the rest of humanity.

And yet ... there was Guy. Guy, who was also Nick. The other Nick, revealed not even to Christopher but only to Christopher's invented self. Guy could be vulnerable; could admit to despair, and to uncertainties. In the partnership of Guy and Oliver, it was Oliver who was strong, stable, without problems. In their angst-ridden sessions together, it was always Guy who did the suffering.

Looking back, as he sat in the churchyard, Christopher found he could scarcely remember a time when soul-searching and harrowing mental anguish had not formed the staple of the relationship between Guy and Oliver. In the early days, perhaps; perhaps then it may have been more light-hearted. Vague recollections drifted shadowlike across his memory. Mental images, brief and flitting ... Guy's first concert, Oliver's first book ... 'Brilliant Young Pianist', 'Writer of Promise' ... TV chat shows, Desert Island Discs ... 'And if you could take only one record with you?' Guy choosing Elgar, Oliver choosing – what? He couldn't remember what Oliver had chosen; it seemed so long ago. But it was all there on tape, if ever they needed it.

Of course, it had still been a game in those days; a game at which they had play-acted. The difference between then and now was that the game had ceased to be a game. They had outgrown mere play-acting. These days, in the privacy of Nick's room they actually assumed the mantle of their own creations: for long stretches of time they became their fantasies.

It was not an ability which had been granted them overnight; rather it had crept upon them gradually, with stealth, taking them unaware. In the beginning it had necessitated a conscious act of will – 'And Guy would say, and Oliver would reply.' These days they could slip straight in with no preliminaries. Christopher could even do it by himself, tucked away beneath the duvet late at night or in the early morning. He could be Guy, he could be Oliver, just as he chose. He didn't know whether Nick was able to do this; he had never

17

asked. To indulge their habit was one thing, openly to admit it, quite another.

The game they played now was keeping up the myth that Guy and Oliver were but fictitious characters in the Great Novel they one day planned to write. To this end, they were scrupulously methodical. Locked away in Nick's desk they had a complete and complicated filing system: comprehensive records listing everything they had ever invented, from detailed family trees down to school reports and birth certificates. They had spent the whole of one Christmas compiling and arranging their records, because over the years the original world of make-believe had developed into a whole community, still centred on the main figures of Our Heroes but containing too many subsidiary characters, too many minor details for their memories to handle with comfort. It was essential to keep the fictional world as plausible as they could. It tended to destroy the reality of it if people kept changing their religion, or the colour of their eyes, with the same regularity with which, in real life, they changed their houses and their cars.

So Christopher sat in the churchyard, his back against the yew, surrounded by graves, by ancient tombstones, overgrown and crumbling, and considered what might happen if Oliver were to become a Catholic. Or possibly a lapsed Catholic.

He was still undecided whether to take the final step and commit himself when the church clock struck the hour, and he remembered that the coach had been due to leave fifteen minutes ago. Louise would be panicking, imagining murder and rape. His grandmother would be clicking her teeth and telling everyone that it was 'Typical of that boy . . . typical!'

Unfortunately, in this case, she happened to be right.

2

'There's a letter come for you,' said Louise.

'Where from?' He spoke with his head muffled beneath the duvet. She wasn't getting him up that easily. Last time she had held out the lure of a letter it had been nothing but a printed form from the library reminding him that one of his library books was overdue.

Louise yanked at the curtains. 'From abroad.'

From Nick. He shot up the bed, clutching the duvet round him. She obviously must know that it was from Nick; nobody else wrote to him from abroad. So why not say so? Why not say, 'From Nick?' Because she didn't approve of him being friends with Nick, that was why not. Nick was too clever and his family were too rich, and he made her feel inferior.

'May I have it?' He held out a hand. Louise, with a slight pursing of the lips, as if it were something mildly distasteful, dropped the letter on to his bedside table.

'I'm off to work now.'

'OK.'

She stood watching him, from the door. Why couldn't she just go? He wasn't opening Nick's letter while she was there.

'You don't want to be late,' he said.

'I'm not late, Christopher. It's only ten o'clock.' Louise worked part-time, ten-thirty to four-thirty, in a local eating place. (The Merrie Kettle; you couldn't really call it a restaurant. It was where people like his grandmother went for morning coffee and cream cakes.) 'You're the one who's late.' She continued to stand, just inside the door. 'Your gran said it was lunchtime, yesterday, before you made a move.'

'I had a headache.'

'I'm not surprised you had a headache, stuck there under the duvet. I don't know what you think you're going to do when you go back to school on Monday. I'm not going to keep shouting up the stairs at you.'

'When I have to get up, I'll get up.' He was supposed to be on *holiday*. He bet Nick wasn't nagged like this. But then probably, in Switzerland, there'd be something worth getting up for. What was there in Holt Wood? It was almost as bad as Smeaton. 'Anyway,' he said, 'I didn't turn the light out till two o'clock. I was reading.'

'That's your problem,' said Louise.

What did she mean, that was his problem? He sat up reading because he enjoyed sitting up reading. That didn't give him any problem. It might give *her* a problem. But that was her problem; not his. He started to explain it to her, but as usual she cut him short.

'I can't stand here listening to you all day. Some of us have work to do.'

Louise thumped off down the stairs, leaving his bedroom door ajar in a clumsy attempt at galvanizing him into action. She knew he couldn't stand to be in his bedroom with the door open. He turned, wrenched a pillow from beneath his elbow and hurled it across the room. The door banged shut. There was a second's

20

pause, then predictably, his grandmother's voice from the hallway: 'How many times has that boy been told not to slam the door? He'll bring the house down!'

If people wouldn't leave doors open, there wouldn't be any need to slam them. He lay back again, minus pillow, to open his letter. It wasn't a letter, in fact, but a card. On Christopher's instructions, Nick always sent his postcards in an envelope. It was to stop his grandmother reading them. Christopher's grandmother, that was; not Nick's. He knew that his grandmother read his postcards for he had once caught her at it. Standing there brazenly in the hall, openly reading. (When he had taxed her with it she had said that 'Postcards were for everybody, and anyway he shouldn't have secrets; not from his own family.')

The message on the card was brief. In Nick's bold Italic script, which Christopher envied but was quite unable to imitate (his own was just a scrawling mess), it said, *Back Thurs/Fri. Will ring w/l.*

He was puzzled for a minute by *w/l*. He might have fantasised that it stood for 'with love', except that he and Nick were not in the habit of exchanging endearments. Love did not come into it (whatever some people might think). Intellectual companionship was what it was about: a meeting of true minds. He supposed, if pushed, they would admit to a degree of affection, yet he wasn't even sure about that. Nick wasn't the sort to be emotional; very sparing with his feelings, was Nick. They were each other's closest friend, indeed each other's only friend. The relationship was one of total exclusion, rigorous in its demands of absolute loyalty, absolute commitment; but love did not come into it.

He lay back against the headboard, cudgelling his brains. With? When? when . . . landed! Of course! Nick always called him from the airport. He wondered what flight he would be on. He usually arrived somewhere around mid-afternoon or early evening, though once it had been as late as nine p.m. and Louise had made a fuss about Christopher travelling up to Waterloo to meet him. That had been when he was only fourteen, though she'd probably still make a fuss, if only as a matter of principle. She really hated him being friends with Nick.

Downstairs the telephone started ringing. He waited for someone to answer it, but both Louise and his grandmother must have sneaked out silently while he was still pondering the meaning of Nick's cryptic abbreviations. Let it ring; it wouldn't be for him. It *could* be for him. Today was Thursday: it could be Nick, arriving on an early flight. Dragging the duvet with him, he jumped naked out of bed and went hopping down the stairs.

'Hello?'

It wasn't Nick, it was some woman wanting his grandmother. He said, 'She's not here at the moment. She's gone out.'

'Oh. Is that Christopher?'

Guardedly he agreed that it was. He didn't like becoming involved in conversations with his grandmother's acquaintances; he was never too sure what she might have told them about him.

'This is Helen Sanderson here. I don't expect you'll remember . . . we all came to visit you, just before we left for Australia. Helen and Mel? With Glenn and Sarah? It probably doesn't mean anything to you.'

He made a vague mumbling noise. She was right, it didn't mean a thing. His memory for events which had taken place in his infancy was highly selective. Mostly what he remembered was his grandmother nagging at him.

He took down a telephone number, in Salisbury, and a message for his grandmother to 'give me a call when she gets in' and shuffled through to the kitchen in his duvet in search of breakfast. Two pieces of leathery toast had been thrown in the bin. He toyed with them for a moment, decided in the end that it wasn't worth the effort of getting the marge out and spreading them, snatched a glass of milk and a fungicidal apple and loped back up the stairs to consume them in the privacy of his bedroom.

He supposed he had better make at least a minimal effort of clothing himself. You never knew, some idiot could always come banging on the door, wanting to read the meter or talk about the Bible. It was never anything of the least importance, but they got mad at him if he just lay there in bed and did nothing. Like on Tuesday when someone had come to service the water heater and had pushed a card through the box saying *Our Engineer called at eleven-forty-five a.m. but was unable to gain admittance.* Louise had been quite narked.

'Lying there in bed at quarter to twelve!'

He had tried saying he must have been in the garden, but they hadn't believed him. What would he have gone in the garden for, on a soaking wet day? What did he ever go in the garden for?

'I should very much doubt,' Louise had said bitterly, 'if you even knew what the garden *looks* like.'

Of course he knew what it looked like! He spared it a glance through his bedroom window as he put some Shostakovich on the record player. It was small and square and sodden. It had a small square sodden patch of grass, surrounded on three sides by small sodden flowerbeds containing an assortment of small sodden flowers. It had looked the same ever since he could remember. There really didn't seem to be very much point in going out into it.

He ate his apple to the satisfying braying of Shostakovian brass, moderated the volume and settled down to do some work on one of his projects. He had finished all the official ones, for school, weeks ago: they were piled up neatly on a shelf. His own personal projects he kept strictly under lock and key, in a briefcase he had bought for the purpose at a local jumble sale. He didn't think that Louise would ever go prying amongst his possessions, not without some pretty radical excuse (like convincing herself he was on drugs); she tended on the whole to respect his privacy, apart from her early-morning incursions when he was still half-asleep. It was his grandmother he didn't trust, at home all day with time on her hands and a quite obsessive conviction that he was up to no good.

'What's he do all the time, locked away in that bedroom? It's not natural . . . boy of his age.'

He unlocked the briefcase and spread the contents over his desk, wondering which he felt most in the mood for. Number 1 was his novel. He had written five chapters of the novel and then come to a fullstop. It was called *The Paper Harpsichord* and was rather high-flown; he wasn't sure any more that he knew what it was meant to be about.

He put *The Paper Harpsichord* to one side, likewise a folder marked POETRY (he was a bit depressed about his poetry: he couldn't stop writing like W.H. Auden) and another labelled RESEARCH. Research was an ongoing project in which he noted down pieces of useful information, various fatuous and bigotted remarks

24

uttered by his grandmother, snippets of interesting conversation overheard on buses, plus his own cynical reflections on the nature of society – 'Everybody who is anybody has always been somebody' was one which had recently come to him. He was thinking of making a poster of it and hanging it over his bed.

Only two folders now remained. On the front of one was written *Book of Great British Turds*, or, in brackets, *Turds of Great Britain*. He and Nick had thought this particular project up between them one day last Easter. The idea was to produce a coffee-table book full of glossy photographs of different kinds of turds in different locations – 'Seagull turd on Smeaton Beach', 'Common dog turd, Holt Wood High Street' – interspersed at intervals with photographs of prominent public figures such as Margaret Thatcher and Jeffrey Archer. So far they had drawn up a list of forty-eight prominent figures plus a handful of captions for the as yet non-existent photographs. Christopher didn't have a camera, and Nick, who had, seemed rather to have gone off the idea, which was a pity. He reckoned it could have earned them a fortune. It would also have upset his grandmother and maybe have brought interviews on local radio. Still, it wasn't any use without Nick. It was the sort of thing you either did together or not at all. Photographing turds by oneself would be decidedly kinky.

Reluctantly, he put *Turds of Great Britain* back into his briefcase. That left only one: *Titillating Tales* (full title: *Titillating Tales for Toddlers*) by Christopher Seymour and Nicholas Sheringham. If Roald Dahl could get rich on *Revolting Rhymes*, he really didn't see why he and Nick couldn't do likewise with *Titillating Tales*. He opened it up at the last page.

Christopher Robin.
Little boy stands at the foot of the bed,
Little hand working, little face red.
Splish, splosh, into the pot,
Christopher Robin has just sh –

From downstairs came the sound of the front door opening. Quickly, he reached for the volume control on the record player and turned it full up. Shostakovich's Sixth symphony roared and howled across the room. He could feel the floor vibrating to the steady thud-BANG of the drum. Satisfied, he went back to his desk: at least now she wouldn't have to come spying on him, checking that he was awake.

'Playing that music, he was ... had the whole house shaking. Couldn't even hear me when I shouted at him. Not surprised, the racket that was going on. Boom, boom, boom.' His grandmother made exaggerated grimaces with her lips across the supper table. She looked like a cod, mouthing at him. 'Goodness only knows what the neighbours must have thought.'

The neighbours wouldn't have thought anything. They were incapable of thought. They were all totally mindless.

He said: 'You can't expect a full symphony orchestra to sound like a tearoom trio.'

'I wouldn't expect it to sound like anything ... not in a person's bedroom. I wouldn't have said, if you'd asked me, that a person's bedroom was the right sort of place to have a full symphony orchestra.'

'So where am I expected to have it? Downstairs in the same room where you're watching television?'

'In a concert hall, I should have said. If you'd asked me.'

'And how am I supposed –'

Louise sighed. She was used to coming home to scenes of conflict. 'Don't argue, Christopher. Your grandmother's quite right. These walls are far too thin for the sort of volume you play things at. You ought to have one of those walk-abouts, then you could just deafen yourself instead of other people.'

'I should think he would deafen himself! Go around like zombies, some of them, plugged into those things. Twitching and carrying on.' Across the table, his grandmother made twitching motions, jerking her shoulders up and down like an old rag doll. 'I'm not surprised there's all this violence . . . spooned out of their minds half the time.'

He was still trying to work out what she meant by spooned when in the hall the telephone started ringing. He shoved back his chair. 'I'll get it!' It could be Nick, calling to say he'd arrived.

'Hello?'

It wasn't Nick, it was the woman who had rung that morning. Helen Sanderson. He had forgotten all about her.

'Who is she?' he said, when his grandmother had gone off to speak to her.

'She's your grandmother's niece,' said Louise. 'She's been living abroad for years . . . Canada or somewhere.'

He didn't like to say 'Australia' in case she asked him how he knew, which would have meant admitting that she'd called earlier and that he'd neglected to pass on the message. He hadn't done it on purpose; it had genuinely slipped his memory.

Maybe, with any luck, the woman wouldn't mention it.

'That was Helen on the phone.' His grandmother had returned, self-important, to the table. 'My niece, Helen. Kathleen's girl. Just got back from Australia. You met her once, Lou, do you remember? Lovely girl. Done ever so well for herself. We always knew she would. If anyone had the brains of the family, it was Helen. Had the looks as well, mind you. I remember –'

Christopher listened, with half an ear – lovely family, charming husband, everybody brilliant. Glenn, Sarah, delightful children, beautiful manners, handsome, talented, everybody wonderful. Nick wasn't very likely to arrive now. He had obviously decided on an extra day. He wondered if he minded Nick having an extra day. Would *he* have had an extra day, if he had been in Nick's position? Or would he selflessly and nobly have thought of poor old Nick, left behind in Holt Wood –

'– think it would be rather nice if you were here.'

'What?' He became aware that his grandmother was talking at him. 'Me? When?'

'When they come round.'

He must have missed something.

'The Sandersons,' said Louise. 'They're coming over on Saturday.'

'You shouldn't have to repeat things to him. He ought to pay attention when people are speaking. Never listens to a word anyone says.'

'I was listening,' said Christopher. 'I just blacked out for a second.'

'Blacked out?' said Louise. A note of alarm had come into her voice. His grandmother sniffed.

'Losing his hearing, more like. All that racket he makes up there ... music, he calls it! I call it a nasty tuneless row. Of course, I wasn't educated to it. I realize that. Didn't have the benefits some people are getting.'

Christopher opened his mouth, but Louise was there first.

'What we want to know is whether you're going to be in on Saturday?'

The answer to that was no. If Nick were arriving back tomorrow they would spend Saturday up in town, looking round the bookshops, going to a concert. She knew that. She knew very well that he always spent the last weekend of the holidays doing things with Nick.

'They'll expect it,' said his grandmother. 'They're coming all the way from Salisbury.'

'Not to see me.'

'Not you specially, no. I can't imagine anyone coming to see you specially. Not with the sort of manners you've got. But it's only polite you should be here.'

'So could you, do you think?' said Louise. 'Could you at least manage to be here for lunch? Just to say hello?'

'Yes, and that's another thing!' Out of the blue, his grandmother pounced. 'Couldn't even pass on a simple message, could he? Couldn't even tell me that Helen had already rung. Even left her telephone number for him to give me. All that expensive education and couldn't even be trusted to perform a simple task like that ... wouldn't be much good relying on *you* in a matter of life and death!'

He spent all the following day skulking indoors, waiting for the telephone to ring. His grandmother, who seemed to have some kind of sixth sense where such things were concerned, also spent the day skulking indoors; but while Christopher skulked in his bedroom, she skulked in the kitchen, with the result that on the three occasions when the telephone actually came to life she managed to beat him to it.

On the first occasion it was one of her whist cronies. Someone called Win. He hung about on the landing, listening as his grandmother engaged in a long rambling conversation to do with conspiracy and intrigue down at the whist club.

'It's that new lot,' she said. 'Far too clicky for my liking.'

He wondered what she meant by clicky. He went back to his room to brood over it and had just reached the conclusion that it must come from *clique* when once again the telephone rang. He burst out on to the landing even as his grandmother was lifting the receiver. She must have been waiting by it, like some great hover fly. She said, 'Yes?' And then, 'No, it's not,' and slammed the receiver back down. Her usual way of dealing with wrong numbers. She always took them as some form of deliberate insult.

After that, there was silence for several hours. It was four o'clock when next it rang. This time it *had* to be Nick. He catapulted out of his room and down the stairs, reaching the telephone at precisely the same moment as his grandmother.

They stood, looking at each other; then his grandmother stretched out a hand. She picked up the receiver. Very slow and deliberate, to keep him waiting. She said, 'Hello?' And then, after a long pause: 'What was it you were after, exactly?' Another pause; even longer. It had to be Nick. She was doing it on purpose. Pretending not to recognize him, not to understand. 'Thank you,' she said. 'But not today.'

She hung up.

'So who was that?' he said.

She waited till she was halfway down the hall. 'Someone about fitted kitchens.'

She liked nothing better than to thwart him.

At nine o'clock that evening he went downstairs to watch the television news. His grandmother, of course, had to remark on it: 'My! We are honoured. I'm surprised you can bear to lower yourself.'

He stayed for the full half-hour, but nothing was said about any disasters, road, rail, air or otherwise. He had to assume that something else had occurred. Maybe the flight had been delayed, diverted . . . hijacked? No, they would have said.

'I hope you didn't find it too demeaning . . . coming down to our level for a change.' His grandmother leaned forward, complacent, to switch channels. 'I'm sorry we couldn't offer you anything more exciting. No nice juicy scandals. No catastrophes. If you'd joined us yesterday you could have seen some earthquake victims, you'd have liked that.'

'I have no desire,' he said loftily, 'to look at earthquake victims.'

'Well, you ought to have. Boy of your age, ought to keep abreast of what goes on in the world.'

'One can keep abreast of world affairs without resorting to voyeurism.'

'Oh, there we go again with our clever French words! Don't know why you bothered coming down at all if you've got no interest in what's going on . . . I suppose you'll be back off upstairs now, bury your nose in a book.'

'I happen,' he said, 'to have work to do.'

'Yes, I've heard that one before.'

*

He spent half the night lying awake sweating, convinced that Nick was dead. (What would he *do*? Without Nick?) By eight o'clock next morning he was down in the kitchen, fully dressed, frantically re-tuning the radio from Radio 3, which was where he liked to leave it to annoy his grandmother, across the dial to LBC, for the news. No disasters, it appeared, had happened during the hours of darkness – but if it had been a local disaster, in Switzerland, they wouldn't necessarily report it, would they? He snatched up the *Daily Mail* and was furtively flipping through the pages to the foreign news when Louise appeared.

'My, you're up bright and early,' she said.

He grunted, stuffing the paper behind him on to a chair. 'Getting in training for next week.'

'Good! I'm glad to hear it. Do you want some toast?' She had seen him, looking at the *Mail*, but she didn't make any crass remarks about deigning to lower himself, or slumming it. She wasn't snide like his grandmother. On the other hand she did sometimes show herself a bit more clued into the state of his mind than he altogether liked. She said now, as she lit the grill: 'Isn't it about time you heard from Nick? I should have thought he'd be back by now.'

He mumbled, 'Today, I expect.'

'Well, if you could just be around to say hello to these relatives . . . I know your gran would appreciate it. They'll be arriving about eleven, so –'

Nick could call at any moment. If he'd been in the house alone he would have tried ringing his parents; see what had gone wrong. He wasn't going to do it with his grandmother around, he knew she always listened in on his telephone conversations; and if Louise by chance overheard she would guess that he was worried. He always took care never to display any weakness in front of his mother. It made him too vulnerable, and besides it compromised his dignity.

After breakfast he said, 'I'm just going up the road for a paper. I'll only be five minutes.' He said that in case Nick should ring while he was gone.

There was a public call box on the corner of Ridgemount Road and Dalmally. He dialled Nick's number, the receiver clamped in clammy hand, backs of his knees already prickling. He hated speaking to Nick's parents. His father never seemed to know who he was, his mother seemed always to be pissed. But he would still rather speak to either of them than to Gerald. Gerald was Nick's brother. He had been in the sixth when Christopher had started at Astley and had since become something sordid on the Stock Exchange. Rightly or wrongly, he always had the feeling that Gerald despised him.

As it happened, it wasn't any of the family who answered, but the Swedish au pair. She said, 'I am sorry, there is nobody here. Will I pass on the message?' She spoke in a strange, guttural sing-song. He was never quite sure how much the succession of au pairs who seemed to run the Sheringham household actually understood of the English language. Carefully he said, 'Can you tell me if Nick is back from Switzerland yet, please?'

Nick was not back; there had been a delay. His immediate surge of relief was almost instantly swamped by a fresh wave of agitation: what sort of delay?

The delay, it appeared, was Nick's grandmother. 'She is not well. It is her heart and Nick must stay with her.'

'So when –' Christopher swallowed. He wiped a sweaty palm down the seat of his jeans. 'I mean, h-how long –'

'I am sorry; I cannot tell. One week, maybe. Two weeks, maybe.'

Christopher replaced the receiver and stumbled out, on jellified legs, into Dalmally Road. Already he could feel the familiar panic spreading through him. If Nick were to be a fortnight late coming back – right at the beginning of term – the beginning of a new year – the very worst time of all. The long, lonely wastes of the first day, before timetables were organised – the hours and hours that stretched between one period and another – it wasn't possible! He couldn't face it! Days when Nick were absent were unendurable. They were a torture worse than any physical pain he could imagine. Nick was the sole friend he possessed. Without Nick –

He stopped. There was a car parked outside the house. People were climbing out of it. A man, a woman, and a moon-faced girl. Even as he watched, they all went trooping in through the gate and up the garden path. He saw the front door open and his grandmother appear, nodding and beaming.

It was them. They had got there early. And now he had no option but to spend the day fraternising.

3

They had only brought Sal with them. Glenn, Helen Sanderson explained, had gone off to a cricket match: 'We didn't have the heart to drag him away.'

He resented the unknown Glenn being allowed to absent himself. He looked across at his grandmother to see how she was taking it, but she refused to meet his eye. He wasn't surprised. All that fuss they had made! *You will be here, Christopher, won't you? They'll expect to see you, Christopher. It's only polite, Christopher.* He could have gone up to town by himself. Not that he would have done, probably; he didn't really care for going without Nick. It was the principle of the thing.

Helen Sanderson had brought along a photograph of Christopher in short trousers at the age of eight. He was sitting on an upturned bucket in the back garden with a little wooden spade in his hand. Sitting next to him, on another upturned bucket, was a small fat gnome in a boiler suit. The fat gnome, whom he at first assumed to be Glenn, turned out in fact to be the girl, Sarah.

He glanced at her covertly across the room. (They had chosen, by common agreement it seemed, to sit as far away from each other as was possible within the confines of a small suburban sitting-room.) From time to time he noticed that she was directing the same covert glances at him. She had a long straggling fringe of brownish-coloured hair which fell into her eyes, so that she was forever poking it aside with her fingers or tossing her head to get it out of the way. Whenever she poked or tossed she would take the opportunity to dart a quick look at him.

It made him self-conscious. It wasn't even as if he'd dressed for the occasion: just his ordinary everyday sweatshirt and jeans. The sweatshirt could well be a bit niffy, he'd been wearing it for over a week, and the jeans had rude words scribbled on both legs. Even as he sat there he could quite clearly see the words BALLS staring up at him from his right thigh. Surreptitiously, he picked up his left foot and placed it over the offending word. The only way he could get his foot to stay in position was by jamming it into his crutch. It was like some kind of mad yoga pose. It was also extremely uncomfortable. Not to say painful.

He shifted his buttocks, trying to redistribute his body weight. From across the room, the girl shot him a distinctly mischievous glance through a gap she had just made in her fringe. Was she laughing at him?

He scowled, unjammed his foot, crossed his legs at the ankles and prudishly placed his hands over himself. Sarah shook her hair back into her eyes and retired again behind her fringe. Unlike him, she had gone to the trouble of dressing up – well, he supposed it would be called dressing up. She was wearing a short flouncy skirt showing all her legs and a black off-the-shoulder top which looked to him as if it might at any moment descend to being rather more than off-the-shoulder. (He

36

imagined it happening and went hot with embarrassment. Where would one look? What would one do?)
She had slimmed down since the day they had sat on
their upturned buckets to have their photographs taken,
but she was still a bit on the plump side – 'Well covered,'
as his grandmother would say, in tones of approval.

Christopher wasn't sure whether he approved or
not. He wasn't sure of anything very much where girls
were concerned. He didn't think she could be described
as pretty. Her face was too round and too bland and the
limp hair didn't help, just hanging about all anyhow. On
the other hand she wasn't positively *un*-pretty. There
had been a moment, just a fleeting moment, when she
had peered through her fringe at him, when she had
struck him as being almost attractive.

'Christopher –' Helen Sanderson had suddenly left
her place on the sofa and was coming over to him. 'Why
don't you and I swop seats? Then you and Sal could sit
and talk. I'm sure it would be far more interesting for
you than having to listen to us old folk.'

Presented with a *fait accompli*, there wasn't very
much that he could do. He could hardly say he was
quite happy where he was and send her back again.

He shambled, head down and pigeon-toed, across
the room. Sarah gave him a quick grin and bunched
up her skirt so that he could sit down without crushing
it. He racked his brains for something to say. His grandmother was nearby, easily within hearing distance. He
knew she'd be straining to catch what was going on.
(She'd report it afterwards to her friends: 'Oh, I did
laugh! Hear Christopher, trying to make conversation
to a girl for the first time in his life.') But you
couldn't just sit in silence. Oliver wouldn't. He had
had the advantages of a Good Upbringing: he was never

at a loss. What would he say now, if he were here? He leaned back, casually, trying to be Oliver.

'So how was Australia?' he said. His voice came out low, and erotically husky. It sounded almost indecent; as if he were putting some kind of lewd sexual suggestion to her.

Sarah said, 'Hot!' and giggled.

'H–' he scraped at his throat – 'hot all the time?'

'Not all the time.' She giggled again. 'Just most of the time.'

'I don't think I should like that,' he said.

'Don't you?' said Sarah.

He waited a bit.

'Did you?' he said.

'I didn't mind.'

'I suppose you get acclimatized.'

'I s'pose.'

Riveting. They were almost having a Real Conversation. He struggled to recall what little he knew of Australia. *And tell me, my dear . . .*

'Did you see the Great Barrier Reef?'

'Yes,' she said. 'And the outback. And the sheep.'

Of course, she must have been asked the same stupid questions a thousand times since getting back. If he had been Oliver he could have said, 'And the koalas?' and then she would have said, 'And the koalas,' and it would have been like a sort of joke between them; but he wasn't Oliver, and so he didn't.

A long, painful pause settled on them. Sarah pulled a strand of hair into her mouth and began chewing at it. Christopher looked at the floor and saw again the word emblazoned on his thigh. He rubbed at it with a finger. He rubbed until the finger was sore and his thigh, beneath his jeans, red hot with friction. Sarah, chewing on her hair, sat watching him. It occurred to him, suddenly, that what he was doing looked incredibly vulgar. He stopped at once and crossed his legs again.

'Where would you rather live?' he said. 'England, or Australia?'

'I don't really mind,' she said. 'I'm happy wherever I am.'

'You wouldn't say that if you lived in Holt Wood,' he said. He only said it for the benefit of his grandmother.

'We might be going to, soon,' said Sarah. 'My dad's got the offer of a job, up in London. We were talking on the way over about maybe coming to live here.'

He said, 'In Holt Wood?' The idea faintly alarmed him, he didn't know why.

'It's supposed to have everything,' said Sarah. 'Shops; schools; green belt. Near to London. All the things that people want.'

He was flabbergasted. 'Who told you that?'

'Your grandmother,' she said. 'The other night, on the phone, when she was talking to Mum.'

It was a ploy! A dastardly ploy. No one in their right mind could possibly claim that Holt Wood had all the things that people wanted. Not unless they were vegetables. Where was the theatre? Where was the cinema? Where was the concert hall, the museum, the art gallery?

'Don't you like it here?' said Sarah.

Like it? 'There isn't anything *to* like.'

She shook her head, as one bewildered by, but prepared nonetheless to show compassion for, a fellow human's disability. 'What about schools?'

'What about them?'

'What's the one you go to?'

39

He said, 'Astley College, actually,' without quite knowing why he tacked on the actually except that it seemed somehow to finish the sentence. Or maybe it was intended as an apology for the fact that it was the sort of school that it was. Not that he had been responsible for choosing it. He just went where he was told to go.

Sarah said, 'Oh, yes! That's right. Your grandmother told us. She said they ought to try and get Glenn in there. Do you have to be terribly clever?'

'Depends,' he said. 'Not if you can afford to pay.'

It sounded like a put-down; he hadn't meant it to be. What he had really been trying to say was that the only reason he was there was because of getting the scholarship. He felt it absolved him of some of the social guilt attached.

Sarah said, 'Well, they both work so I should think they probably could.'

He said, 'Oh. Right.' And then, as an afterthought: 'Right.'

'The thing is, Glenn needs to pull his finger out, Dad says.'

'Really?'

'He's not what you'd call studious. Not like you. You're very studious, aren't you? Your grandmother said.'

Angrily, he denied it: 'I'm not *very* studious.'

She looked at him, doubtfully. 'Aren't you?'

'No, I'm not!'

'She said you were.'

'Well, I'm not.' There were times when he loathed his grandmother, making him out to be some kind of freak.

Sarah said, 'Well, anyway, you're obviously more studious than Glenn.'

There really wasn't any reply to that. The conversation, such as it had been, dwindled awkwardly into another silence. Sarah picked at a spot on her chin; Christopher took off his shoe and put it back on again. To his horror, into the void came the voice of his grandmother: 'Why don't you take Sarah upstairs and show her your things?'

Sarah giggled, and retreated hastily behind her fringe. Christopher, having no such refuge, looked down at the floor. All he could see was the word BALLS writ large on his thigh. He felt his cheeks erupt into instant nettle rash. There were times when his grandmother was really quite unspeakably dreadful.

Mel Sanderson, taking pity on him, said: 'I understand you've got quite a record collection up there. Sal's a great one for the music.'

'Yes, but just remember,' said Louise. She put a finger to her lips. 'The neighbours . . .'

'Oh! You have that trouble too, do you?' That was Helen Sanderson, leaning forward eagerly. 'Heavy metal blaring out at about a million decibels into the small hours?'

Louise looked dubious: she obviously didn't know what heavy metal was. His grandmother said, 'That's exactly what it sounds like . . . dustbin lids.'

Mel Sanderson jerked his head towards the door. 'Go on! Off you go. And just keep it at a reasonable level.'

Christopher trailed across the room followed by Sarah, sucking at her hair.

'Lunch in half an hour!' called Louise.

Sarah didn't like any of his records; he had known that she wouldn't. She screwed up her nose and said, 'Ugh! Grot! They're all classical.' Then she looked at his books and said, 'We had to do that, last year.' She pointed at *Middlemarch*. 'Dead boring.' It had never occurred to him that a person could find *Middlemarch* boring. It had obviously never occurred to her that anyone could find it anything else.

'Most of that old stuff's a bore. Don't you think?'

Not wishing to appear studious, he didn't answer her directly but said: 'So who's your favourite writer, then?'

'Don't really know ... haven't really got one. Danielle Steel, maybe? I read her. D'you read her?'

He shuffled nervously.

'And Agatha Christie,' she said. 'I've read all Agatha Christie. And Jackie Collins. Have you read Jackie Collins?'

Fortunately, before he was forced into answering, something else had caught her eye. 'What's this?' She went on tiptoe to peer at last year's school photograph, stretched out, scroll-like, above the mantelpiece, secured to the wall with Blu-Tack. (He had stuck it up there for use as a dartboard but hadn't yet got around to actually aiming any darts at it.) 'Which is your form? Show me where your form is! I'll see if I can recognize you.'

Reluctantly he pointed out last year's upper fifth, gawking in the back row like a load of goons. She spotted Christopher almost at once. He was doing his usual squinting act, face screwed up as if in agony.

'Was the sun in your eyes? Or had you just eaten school dinner? Hey, look at this fat guy! And this funny one here with the pointed head ... he must have something wrong with him. And this one at the end!' She went into sudden convulsions. 'Look at his *hands*!' Christopher looked at the hands in question and wondered what was wrong with them. They just looked like ordinary hands to him. '*Ug*,' said Sarah. 'Who's this one? He's not bad.'

'Harry Morgan.' A nerd. A brainless uncultured nerd. He never knew what girls saw in these great lumbering barrel-chested types.

'And this one –'

Andy Robson; another nerd. But reputed to have a way with him. Hence his nickname: 'Randy Robson'.

'*Randy?*' She looked at him, delighted. 'Is that what you call him? Or is that what he is?'

He swallowed. Perhaps he oughtn't to have said that. He didn't know how old she was. Fourteen? Fifteen? Did girls know about that sort of thing at that age? He didn't know anything about girls. There had once been talk of introducing them into the sixth form at Astley, on the grounds that they would be a civilizing influence, but nothing so far had come of it.

'Who's this?'

He followed the direction of her finger, stabbing at the photograph. 'That's Nick.'

'Who's Nick? Is he a friend of yours?'

His only friend.

'He looks OK. He looks quite reasonable. Is he? I mean, in real life? Is that what he actually looks like?'

He moved in closer to study Nick's photograph. 'Yes; I suppose so.'

'Well, you ought to know,' she said, 'if he's your friend.'

'It's difficult, when you see people every day.' You stopped noticing. If anyone had asked him, what does Nick look like? he would have been hard put to say. He was tall, he was slim, he was dark – that was about as far as he could go. He didn't have bad breath or acne, or curvature of the spine, or knock knees or a receding chin, so yes, he guessed that all in all he could be described as quite reasonable. Louise, once, had referred to him as 'that rather good-looking boy'. But that had been before she had taken against him. Before she had decided that he was a bad influence.

'Is he nice?' said Sarah.

Most people probably wouldn't have said so. Most people – Harry Morgan, Andy Robson, Louise, his grandmother – would have said he was reserved and aloof. But they only knew him in his ordinary everyday manifestation: Nick the superior, shunning the world. They didn't know him as Oliver knew him.

'Is he?' said Sarah.

'He is when you get to know him.'

'Hm . . .' Sarah came down, thoughtfully, on to her heels. 'He looks a bit like Rik Harper.'

He gave it a beat, then said: 'Rik who?'

She giggled. 'Rik Harper!'

It became obvious that Rik Harper was someone he ought to have heard of. Ought to have done, and hadn't. He didn't like to expose his ignorance by asking her who he was. These gaps in his knowledge had, of late, started to embarrass him. They didn't matter when he was with Nick, because Nick had the same gaps. What Nick said was, who needs to know? But you did need to know, if you wanted to communicate with people. Real people – ordinary people. Even that nerd Harry Morgan despised him for being so out of touch. He had said to him, last term, 'You know what your problem is, don't you? You seem to think you exist on a different plane from the rest of us.' He didn't want to exist on a different plane. He would have given anything – well, almost anything – to be able to exist on the same plane. Breathe the same air, speak the same language . . . be acceptable. The reason people like Harry Morgan couldn't stand him was that they reckoned he felt himself a cut above them, but it wasn't true. He didn't. Only when he was with Nick. When he was by himself he just felt a freak.

'Hey! What's this?' She had picked something up from his desk. '*Titillating Tales?*'

Too late, he realized: he had forgotten to lock it away. He lunged at her, making a grab, but she giggled and side-stepped and whisked it out of reach.

'*Splish, splosh, into the pot –*' he lunged again: again she side-stepped – '*Christopher Robin has just shot his lot?*'

Her screech of laughter must have been heard even further away than Shostakovich's Sixth. Red-faced, he snatched the page away from her.

'It's something I'm working on. A study of – of pornography in children's rhymes.'

She didn't believe a word of it. (How could she, when he had even drawn a small, graphic picture to accompany the text? The thought of the small graphic picture made him break out all over . . .)

'Do you want another one? Shall I give you another one?' She forked her fringe out of her eyes. She had the same mischievous glint as she had had downstairs, watching him jam his foot into his crutch. 'Little Jack Horner sat in the corner, Pulling his pudding and pie. With his thumb up his bum –'

He listened, bemused, as from her pink (and presumably virginal) lips spewed forth a load of garbage of the type normally uttered only by the cruder members of the first year, and then only behind locked doors in the downstairs lavatory.

'– he said, what a *bad* boy am I!' She looked at

45

him triumphantly. 'You could put that one in, couldn't you?'

It was a relief to hear Louise calling up the stairs that lunch was ready.

Over lunch his grandmother said, 'So what did you do up there? I didn't hear any dustbin lids.'

It was Sarah, demurely, who said: 'We just looked at photographs and read Christopher Robin.'

Helen Sanderson affected a double take. 'My God! That's almost culture – compared with the sort of stuff she normally reads!'

Through a hole in her fringe, Sarah directed one of her mischievous looks at him across the table.

'I'm afraid,' said her mother, 'that neither of our two is in the least inclined to literature ... Glenn's more into machinery, Sal's a computer freak.'

Sarah said, 'No, I'm not. It's just that some of us have learnt how to handle them ... it's what's known as being *computer literate.*'

'How about you, Christopher?' Mel Sanderson smiled at him, trying to bring him into the conversation. 'Are you into technology, or –'

His grandmother gave a derisive snort. 'Him? He can't even cope with the mechanics of a tin opener!'

It was true, if she was referring to the new electrical device she had recently installed in the kitchen; but she didn't have to go and tell everyone. Sarah giggled again. Her mother said, 'I wouldn't be so quick to laugh if I were you, Sal Sanderson ... I could tell them a little tale about a garlic press –'

He would have liked to hear about the garlic press, but his grandmother had to go and butt in. She said,

'Why do you call her Sal when she has such a pretty name?'

Sarah made a gagging noise. Helen Sanderson laughed. 'Oh, we thought that Sarah was far too elitist for ourself . . . members of the upper classes are called Sarah. We couldn't possibly be called that. In case, you know, we were confused with them. So now we only answer to Sal.'

'Well, I shan't call her Sal. If you think I'm going to call you Sal, you've got another think coming, young lady! I shall call you Sally.'

He could see, from the wrinkling of her brow beneath the fringe, that Sally, as far as she was concerned, was every bit as bad as Sarah.

At the end of lunch they wanted him to take her into town – what they laughably called town – to show her the sights. He said, 'What sights?' When he put it like that, even his grandmother was stumped for a reply. Louise, brightly, said, 'The Caves . . . you could show her the Caves.' The Caves were in Chislehurst, a twenty-minute bus journey away. The thought of spending twenty minutes with her on a bus, not to mention twenty minutes *waiting* for a bus, was terrifying. What would they talk about, all that time?

'You could show me your school,' said Sarah. (He would *call* her Sal, since that was what she wanted, but he couldn't bring himself to think of her as Sal. It was far too familiar.)

'Yes! Show her where Glenn just *might* be going if he can manage to convince them he's not educationally subnormal.'

'If we move here, that is,' said Mel.

'Well, we've got to move somewhere, you can't keep commuting up and down from Salisbury. I'll tell you what, Christopher! See if you can find a suitable house for us. That'll give you an objective.'

'But we'll look at the school first,' said Sarah.

They left the house and walked back up Dalmally Road to the junction with Ridgemount, where he had stood that morning and telephoned to ask about Nick. He said, 'Are you sure you want to go and look at the school?'

'What else could we go and look at?

'We could . . . we could go and look at the park.' There wasn't much in there, other than a patch of mud and a drinking fountain; but anything was better than having to look at school.

Sarah shook her head. 'I want to see this famous place where Rik Harper goes,' she said.

He wished he knew who Rik Harper was. He didn't imagine that Nick would know. Reluctantly, he turned in the direction of Holt Wood Hill. He had no desire to go and look at Astley. Monday morning was going to be quite soon enough. The thought of a new term without Nick there to sustain him was like his worst nightmares come true. How often had he lain awake, torturing himself? Sweating. Wondering . . . what if Nick were to fall under a bus, get a brain tumour, get AIDS? What if his parents were suddenly to emigrate? What would he do, without Nick?

They walked up past the Sandrock, past the Water Tower, and there it was: beloved school. Sarah stood, clutching at the bars of the wrought iron gates, peering through at the broad green sweep of the playing fields, intersected by the main walk – Broad Walk, as they called it, just to be original – up which, on Monday morning, he would be making his way without Nick.

'Posh,' she said.

He supposed it was, compared to the concrete squalor of the comprehensive, down in the valley. If he hadn't been such a smart ass, winning his scholarship, he would have gone to the comprehensive. If he had gone there he might have known who Rik Harper was. He might have been normal: he might have had friends.

'Where does he live?' said Sarah, as they turned back down the hill.

'Who?'

'Rik Harper . . . your *friend*.'

He didn't like the way she emphasized the word. Almost as if she knew – as if his grandmother had been tattling. *Doesn't know anyone, doesn't go anywhere . . .*

'Nickelarse,' said Sarah. 'Does he live in Holt Wood?'

'Just round the corner.'

'What, near here?'

'We can go and have a look, if you want.'

He didn't know why he took her to look at Nick's place. Showing off? *We may live in some crappy 1930s semi, but see where my friends live.* Friend; he only had the one. But anyway, it wasn't that. It was more complicated than simply showing off. Not quite so base. Like when he turned up the volume controls and sent Shostakovich blaring forth into the world, he didn't *just* do it to annoy his grandmother, he also did it because he wanted others to share in his pleasure. That was why he had brought her here to look at Nick's place. To share in his pleasure.

As a kid, when sometimes on a Sunday Louise had brought him up to Holt Wood and they had walked past the big houses in Uplands – Marden, Ecclefechan, Burnt Pines, Harefield – it had always been Marden that had caught his attention. Probably what had attracted him most as a small boy had been the monkey puzzle tree in the front garden; only now, when he was older, could he appreciate the finer qualities of the house itself: elegant and gracious, Queen Anne or very early Georgian, with a quiet, ageless dignity, standing at peace amongst rich green lawns and gently colourful flowerbeds, its red brick long since mellowed to a soft pinky-brown. Hard to believe that such serenity could enclose the cold, calculated war that went on behind the sun-softened walls; yet he knew that it was so. For all its beauty, Marden was not a happy house.

Sarah leaned over the gate. She forked her fringe out of her eyes. 'Cor!' She said it jokingly, but he could tell she was impressed. 'You sure he really isn't Rik Harper?'

'I'll ask him,' he said.

She giggled. She did a lot of giggling. It wasn't altogether unpleasant, though at times he found it a bit unnerving. 'Imagine if he was and he'd kept it a secret all these years!'

He said, 'Yeah!' and gave a little laugh just to show that he was clued in.

'What do his parents do?'

'His father's a surgeon.'

'What about his mother?'

'His mother isn't anything.' Just a mother. Or maybe not even that. Louise was always somewhat scathing on the subject of Nick's mother. 'Can't see her ever changing a nappy,' she'd say, as if changing nappies were the very apex of motherhood. 'Can't see her ever mopping up sick.'

'I suppose –' Sarah said it thoughtfully – 'I suppose she can afford not to be anything. But I wouldn't want to be. Not even if I married a millionaire. Can you imagine just staying home looking after children all day?'

Nick's mother didn't stay home looking after children. It was one of the things which Louise held against her. 'That poor boy,' she'd say, pretending to be sorry for Nick. (She wasn't really sorry for him. She just felt guilty because of disliking him, when all he did was make her feel inferior.) 'Poor boy doesn't know what it is to have a normal home life.' And then his grandmother would chime in: 'It just goes to show, money isn't everything.'

They wandered slowly back again, past the big houses, back towards the Sandrock. They had just reached Ecclefechan, with its turrets and its pinnacles – all it lacked was a drawbridge – when a small green sports car came rocketing round the corner at 60 mph. He grabbed at Sarah, dragging both her and himself out of sight behind the Ecclefechan yew hedge. The car roared on up the road, made a sudden right-angled turn and screeched to a halt outside the gates of Marden. Sarah shook herself free.

'What d'you do that for? It wasn't going to hit us!'

'No, I know it wasn't.'

'So what d'you do it for?'

He mumbled, 'That was Nick's mother.'

'So?'

'So I didn't especially want to be seen by her.'

She stared at him. 'Why not?'

'Just because.'

'Doesn't she like you?'

He shook his head, impatiently. It irritated him, when people would keep asking questions that he couldn't answer. He had no idea why he should wish to avoid Nick's mother, who was almost certainly indifferent to him. He just had a vague, troubled feeling that he didn't want it getting back to Nick that he had been there, gawping, with a girl. There was something faintly shameful about it.

He quickened his pace, anxious to reach the corner and be back on the neutral territory of the main road. Sarah did a little skip to catch up with him.

'Is she a snob, or something?'

Why did they always have to keep on so? She was as bad as Louise and his grandmother. His grandmother, specially. Of course, he had to remember that Sarah was related. Nosiness was obviously an inheritable trait.

'Would she rather he wasn't friends with you? Because of you being on a scholarship? I've read about things like that. It's the British class system. It's one of the reasons we went to Australia.'

'So what made you come back?' he said. It sounded rude, but he didn't care – and she didn't even seem to notice.

'We came back 'cause Dad's contract expired and he didn't want to renew it. He felt it was time to move on.'

'What's he do, exactly?'

'He's a lecturer,' said Sarah. 'He lectures on economics. And Mum's a teacher. They both really believe in the Value of Education ... that's why they can't understand about Glenn. He told them last term –' she giggled again – 'he wants to be a motor mechanic. They *try* to be broadminded, but they're not terribly good at it. They're really very elitist, only they don't like to admit it. They'd actually be far happier if they had someone like you. They could understand someone like you.'

He wondered, if he had had parents like them – parents who could understand him – whether it would have made any difference. Whether then he would have been able to make friends and be the same as everyone else.

'Where shall we go now?' said Sarah.

'Where do you want to go?'

'Where *is* there to go?'

'Nowhere,' he said.

'There's got to be *somewhere* ... what do you do in the evenings, when you go out? Where do you go then?'

He didn't go anywhere; not unless it was round to Nick's place to listen to music or be Guy and Oliver. He said, 'There's a theatre over in Bromley.'

'What about discos?'

'I don't know about discos.'

'You don't *know* about them?'

'I mean –' he waved a hand – 'I don't go to them.'

'Never?'

'Well – not very often.' Never, actually, would have been nearer the truth; but then she would have thought him a total freak.

'What about parties?'

'Mm –' It came out more negatively than he had intended. She poked aside her fringe. Her eyes widened.

'You don't go to parties *either*?'

'Sometimes.'

She obviously didn't believe him. She had written him off as a boring academic wimp.

'D'you know something?' she said. He looked at her. 'I think it would be *good* for you if Glenn and I came to live here!'

She probably hadn't meant it to sound threatening, but he felt distinctly uneasy.

*

They arrived back in Dalmally Road to find Louise dishing out tea and cakes. Sarah told her parents about seeing Astley, and 'Lots of super houses, up on the hill ... we saw this one where Christopher's friend lives.' She turned to Louise. 'We think his friend is really Rik Harper in disguise!'

Louise smiled and shook her head. He couldn't decide whether she was shaking it because she, like him, had no idea who Rik Harper was – in which case, why couldn't she put him out of his misery and ask? – or whether she simply failed to see the resemblance between Rik Harper and Nick.

'Was that the friend who just rang up?'

The question came from Mel Sanderson. It fell with a clang, into a sudden void: artificially filled by his grandmother clashing plates together on a tray.

'Or was that another one?'

He only had one friend. Christopher turned, slowly, to look at his mother. Louise, flustered, and tinged with a guilty pink, picked up the teapot and began randomly splashing tea into a row of teacups.

'I meant to tell you, Nick rang while you were out. I'm sorry, it completely slipped my memory.'

She had never been a good liar. He knew that if it hadn't been for Mel Sanderson she wouldn't have told him; or at least, not until it was too late. That could mean only one thing. His heart lightened: 'He's back?'

'Yes.' Louise snatched up the milk jug. 'Sarah?'

'Where was he calling from?'

'Helen? – The airport, I suppose. – Milk?'

'Which airport? Heathrow? Or Gatwick?' Even now she was reluctant to give him the details. 'Didn't he say? Didn't he leave a message?'

Louise sighed. 'He said to tell you he'd just got into Heathrow and he'd be making his way to Waterloo.'

'So what time was that?'

'Oh –' She hunched a shoulder. His grandmother, attempting to create a diversion, craftily dropped her piece of cake sticky side up on to the floor.

'Drat!' she said. 'That'll tread in. Christopher –'

'*What time was it?*'

It was Helen Sanderson who told him: 'It must have been about twenty minutes ago.' Louise shifted, uncomfortably. 'Just before you and Sal got back.'

He looked at the clock. If he left straightaway, he could make it. Nick wouldn't jump on the first train at Waterloo; he'd give him a bit of leeway.

'Where are you off to?' said his grandmother. 'You go and get that floor cloth for me.'

'I'll go,' said Sarah.

'It's not up to you to go; you're a guest. He can do it.'

'Christopher,' said Louise. She caught at his arm. In an urgent undertone she said: 'Not now, surely?'

'Why not? I always go and meet him.'

'Yes, but . . . company.'

What difference did company make? Nick had telephoned; he would expect him to be there.

'Habit bound,' said his grandmother. 'You're always complaining about other people being slaves to habit. Just as much a slave as anyone else, I should say. Not to mention total lack of manners.'

'You've got all day tomorrow,' said Louise. 'You just stay where you are and be sociable for once.'

4

A Siberian wind was slicing across the playing field. Christopher dug his hands deep into his pockets, drew his shoulders up to his ears.

'What the hell did we come out here for?'

They were in the sixth form now; no longer juvenile delinquents but 'Young men ... you have become young men! That is how we shall treat you and how we shall expect you to behave.' Being treated as young men meant they could, if they so wished, remain closeted in the sixth form common room during the day's breaks rather than being booted out, willy-nilly, as hitherto, to take air and get exercise.

The only trouble was, Harry Morgan and his mob had taken possession of the common room. They were obsessively playing the latest album by some group called Screaming Virago. They had played it every day for the past ten days. Left to himself, Christopher would cravenly have submitted – anything rather than give fresh cause for irritation and jibes. It had been Nick, arrogantly indifferent, as always, to public opinion, who had finally decreed the noise intolerable and brought them marching out into the Siberian blast of an October gale.

Three weeks into a new term and here they were, walking the Field together during the mid-morning break just as they had walked it all the other mid-mornings for the past – two years? three years? four?

'I've been thinking,' said Nick. With one hand he turned up the collar of his jacket. It gave him the look of someone playing a part in a film. One of those old French films, with people endlessly walking rainswept boulevards in belted mackintoshes and hats pulled over their eyes. Sarah would probably have thought it romantic. 'I've been thinking, about what you said –'

What had he said? ('*You talk such a lot of rubbish, Christopher; you really do.*')

Sarah kept sending him postcards. She had sent him three in the course of the past week. On the first one she had written, *They've definitely decided on Holt Wood!!!* On the second one: *PS They haven't actually found a house yet. But when they do . . . watch out! Here we come!!!* And on the third, which had arrived that morning: *PPS Give my regards to Rik Harper!!!*

'Who is Rik Harper?' Christopher said.

'What?'

'Rik Harper. Who is he?'

'I don't know . . . some moronic pop star.'

'You've *heard* of him?'

'It would be hard not to,' said Nick, 'considering they've got a filthy great poster of the guy all over Weedon's.'

Weedon's was the music store in Bromley where they went to browse every Saturday morning in search of bargain issues and second-hand LPs. Christopher hadn't noticed any posters; but then Nick always did accuse him of walking round with his eyes shut. He made a note to have a look, next time they went in.

'Why, anyway?' said Nick.

'Why what?'

'Why do you want to know?'

'Oh!' He shrugged. 'No reason.' He wasn't telling Nick that a girl called Sal Sanderson thought he was a dead ringer for some pop star. He wasn't sure how Nick would react. He had been pretty sore about Christopher not turning up to meet him that Saturday. Nick didn't understand about the demands made by mothers. Susan Sheringham's policy was live and let live: you go your way, I'll go mine. 'I just heard the name somewhere.'

'Well, anyway —' They turned right, stepping in unison, off the Broad Walk and along Skip Alley — 'what you were saying the other week, about making Oliver RC.'

'Yeah.' He bent his head, which was several centimetres lower than Nick's to begin with, to hide any telltale redness which might invade his cheeks. He was still in those early stages which accompanied any important new discovery about Oliver when even the most casual reference could cause frissons both intensely pleasurable and painfully embarrassing. Like back in the first year when for a short spell he had had a thing about a boy in the upper sixth called Timothy Bicknell. Whenever anyone had said 'Timothy Bicknell' in his presence he had gone bright scarlet. And yet at the same time he had actively done all he could to promote the saying of it, just for the sake of giving himself a secret thrill.

There had been something illicit, something just the tiniest bit shameful, about his feelings for Timothy Bicknell, just as there was something faintly shameful, now, in making Oliver Roman Catholic; religion, he felt, was a kind of weakness. Intellectually quite inde-fensible. To saddle Oliver with a faith was almost akin to giving him a dodgy heart valve or some crippling kind of disease. (He had toyed, in the past, with both possibilities.) Nick, of course, wouldn't see anything shameful about it. He could speak of it quite coolly, quite dispassionately, with absolutely no awareness of the inner tumult it was causing.

'What you were saying, the other week ... I've had a thought.'

'Oh?' He jerked his head up, his attention caught at last.

'I've been wondering,' said Nick, 'whether Guy mightn't train for the priesthood.'

The priesthood ... he savoured it, enjoying the sound of the word, wishing he'd thought of it for himself. Priesthood ... a priest. His friend, Guy ... a priest.

'I'm only wondering,' said Nick. 'It's a big step to take.'

'But not irrevocable.' Priests could always leave the priesthood; become un-priests.

Nick shook his head. 'Not for Guy. Not once he'd committed himself.'

Cold premonitions went slapping over Christopher's grave. 'What about his career?' (What about the life he shared with Oliver?)

'That's something he'd have to think about. It's one of the things which might hold him back.'

'I can't see Guy giving up his career.'

'He wouldn't give up his music. But I'm not sure that a career, as such, would be such a big thing.'

'But what about –' he hesitated – 'celibacy?'

'That wouldn't bother him.'

Nick sounded very certain. Either he had already considered it or dismissed it as not worth considering; Christopher had no idea which of the two it was likely to be. Sex was not a subject they ever discussed in connexion with Guy and Oliver. Once or twice, in the early days, he had attempted it – at the age of fifteen he had been much struck with the notion of Oliver being seduced, while up at university, by an older woman – one of the dons, perhaps – but Nick had seemed to think it infantile. Smut stuff, like kids in the showers. His participation on *Titillating Tales* had only ever been half-hearted; more of an academic exercise than anything else.

'The thing is,' said Nick, 'I wouldn't w–'

He was interrupted by a sudden strangulated shout from somewhere behind: 'Hey! You there!'

They stopped, and turned. Pat MacMaster, new on the staff last year, young and Irish, full of huff and puff and insane enthusiasm for all things school, was belting across the grass in an effort to head them off.

'You! Nick Sheringham!'

Nick froze. Christopher, because he knew him, recognized it as freezing. MacMaster, who didn't, blundered blindly on.

'I want a word with you!'

'With me?' said Nick.

'With you! Yes.' He came to a halt, chest blowing, arms akimbo. Whatever battle it was that he wanted to fight, Christopher could have told him that he had already lost the first round. Nick really couldn't stand people who addressed him as Hey You. Like he couldn't stand it in shops and restaurants when people called him Sonny or Mate. 'Why are you not taking part in my Christmas revue?'

There was a silence.

'I put a notice on the board . . . did you not see the notice I put on the board? *Musicians wanted*. Now, I've all the bass guitars you could possibly ask for, I've even a trombone and a lad that plays the flute. What I don't have is a single, solitary pianist – well, that's a lie! I do have a pianist, in a manner of speaking. In a manner of speaking, I have more pianists than I know what to do with. But it's only a manner of speaking, if you get my drift? What I need is someone who can manage to do a bit more than just plonk up and down the keys –' MacMaster, never one to spare himself in a good cause, energetically plonked on an imaginary keyboard. 'I want a bit more than that. Now, Mr Harrington tells me you're my man – if I can get you.'

MacMaster looked challengingly at Nick, out of blue eyes which popped slightly. Nick might be his man, but he didn't stand a snowball's chance in hell of getting him. His music was something Nick kept strictly private and to himself. Guy was the concert pianist: not Nick. Even in front of Christopher, Nick could rarely be persuaded to sit down and play – only just occasionally, ragging about; never anything serious. He wondered how it was that Evan Harrington had come to recommend him. Evan Harrington was head of the music department, but Nick had never had piano lessons from him, or, indeed, from any other of the music staff. As far as they were concerned he could be just as great a philistine as Harry Morgan and the rest.

'So!' MacMaster rocked forward on the balls of his feet. 'How about it? What do you say?'

'Sorry,' said Nick. 'I'm not really into that sort of thing.'

'What do you mean, *that* sort of thing? You mean because it's a revue? We wouldn't be that snobbish, now, would we? We wouldn't still be putting up the same old barriers? Still *compartmentalizing* . . . pop, jazz, classical . . . man, that's dinosaur mentality! Even the big opera stars, even they're coming down off their pedestals and starting to muck in with the rest of us. *South Pacific*, *West Side Story* . . . they can't get enough of it. And why not? What's Giuseppe Verdi – that's old Joe Green' (he closed an eye at Christopher) 'for the likes of us oicks – what's he got, I'd like to know, that Rodgers and Hammerstein haven't?'

'What has Beethoven got,' said Nick, 'that the Beatles haven't?'

'Well . . . you said it!'

'I once read somewhere,' said Nick, 'that the Beatles were the greatest songwriters since Schubert.'

'Right!' MacMaster, delighted, stuck up a thumb. 'So there you are! There you have it!'

'The only thing is,' said Nick, 'I think statements like that are a load of codswallop.'

'Oh!' MacMaster sank backwards again, on to his heels. 'So you think statements like that are a load of codswallop, do you?'

'Yes,' said Nick. 'I do.'

'In other words, you don't rate the Beatles when it comes to songwriting?'

'I never said that.'

'What, then? You don't agree they *were* the greatest since Schubert?'

'Do you?' Nick looked MacMaster straight in the eye.

'Well –' MacMaster spread his hands. 'I can't get too inflated about it.'

Cop-out, thought Christopher.

'How about if I were to say Jeffrey Archer was the greatest writer since Shakespeare?'

'Ah! Well, now!' MacMaster chuckled, glad to be back on home ground. 'That's a rather different kettle of fish!'

'It's comparing like with unlike. Like Schubert and the Beatles. They have totally different aims – they fulfil totally different functions.'

'Yes – well! That's as may be. We won't make too heavy weather of it. Rest assured, I'm not asking you to come and play *Sergeant Pepper* for me. I've plenty of talented lads to do that. Just don't run away with the idea that a revue is a revue is *ipso facto* an object of derision.'

Now he was trying to impress. Fling in a bit of Latin: show them how erudite we are.

'I'll tell you, any production is what you care to make it ... my revue is no exception. It's up to the people who are in it. Parts of it are intended purely to amuse, parts of it are a bit more serious. And since you're obviously a very serious-minded young man –' Nick, almost visibly, withered. Whatever slender chance MacMaster might have had, he had gone and blown it for sure – 'why, then, I'll leave the choice of music entirely up to you! I can't say fairer than that, now, can I? The plonkers can plonk, and you can play just whatever you care to play. Whatever it is, we'll find a slot for it. We'll fit it in somehow. The fact is, Nick –'

MacMaster turned, forcing them to turn with him. They trod in a phalanx, back towards Broad Walk.

'What I'm aiming to do is produce a fairly – but not entirely! – light-hearted look at music through the ages. We'll have everything from Bach to the Beatles,

Palestrina to pop – Scarlatti, Scriabin, even Screaming Virago!'

He flung that in, presumably, for Christopher's benefit. Christopher turned away slightly, dissociating himself.

'So, you tell me what takes your fancy . . . a bite of Beethoven, a mouthful of Mozart, bit of the old Debuss –'

The facetiousness grated. Christopher knew why he was doing it: it was because he felt uneasy. Nick had that effect on people; even people like MacMaster, normally as thick-skinned as a pickled rhino.

'I'm sorry,' said Nick. 'I'd like to say yes, but it's a question of priorities.'

MacMaster's face, always somewhat florid, darkened to a deep mottle.

'I would have thought the end-of-term production might have come fairly high up on the list.'

Nick said nothing.

'We're all putting a lot of effort into this, you know. We all have other claims on our time.'

'I'm sorry,' said Nick.

The end-of-break buzzer had long since sounded. The Field, now, was almost deserted; only in the far distance a troupe of spindly-legged juniors dressed in regulation shorts and T-shirts scuttled nervously, in bunches, round the perimeter, accompanied by one of the big hairy brutes from the sports faculty.

MacMaster tightened his lips. 'I can see I've been wasting my time on you, Sheringham. They told me I would be – I was foolish enough not to believe them. In my innocence, I'd thought any boy privileged to attend this school would be only too proud to represent it. Obviously I was wrong.'

MacMaster swung on his heel and flounced off across one of the side walks.

'Wanker,' said Nick.

Christopher stared after the angrily retreating figure. 'How come old Harrington knew about you playing the piano?'

'It's what's known as social connexions ... gossip on the golf course.'

It must be one of the very few advantages, Christopher reflected, of not having social connexions. The thought of his grandmother mixing freely with people from school was enough to make his blood run cold.

On Saturday morning, as usual, they went into Bromley to sort through the second-hand stock at Weedon's. Stuart Fordyce, who ran the classical side, had told them last week he was getting in a big new collection – 'Some old boy who's going over to CD. Seems he's got stuff dating right back to the Fifties.' They were hoping to pick up a few bargains. Nick always had far more money to spend than Christopher, in fact Nick's resources seemed almost limitless, but it was an accepted thing between them, at least in theory, that Christopher had equal rights when it came to choosing.

The classical department was down in the basement. As they passed through the main body of the shop, making for the rickety wooden staircase at the far end, Christopher noticed for the first time the poster of Rik Harper. Facially, he did bear a fleeting resemblance to Nick; at any rate, he could see why Sarah had remarked on it. He must remember to reply to her flood of postcards.

After leaving Weedon's, with a *Rite of Spring* which had been Christopher's choice, plus a boxed set of Liszt piano music, which had been Nick's, and a random selection of Shostakovich guaranteed to get the neighbours going, not to mention Christopher's grandmother, they set off on their usual tour of the library and the bookshops. Christopher seized the opportunity, in W H Smith, while Nick was reading bits of *Satanic Verses*, to buy a card for Sarah. He deliberately chose the most hideous one he could find – a colour photograph of the main shopping area. On the back he was going to write, BEWARE! THIS IS THE LOCAL CULTURE. Nick, unfortunately, wandered back to his side as he was still in the queue waiting to pay for it.

'What do you want that thing for?'

He lied, fluently: 'She wanted one to send to these relations.'

'You didn't have to pick anything that repulsive!'

'She won't think it's repulsive; she'll think it shows Bromley at its beautiful best.' Nick just looked at him and shook his head.

That evening, Christopher went round to Nick's to listen to the new records. He almost always went to Nick's rather than Nick coming to Dalmally Road. The walls were thin in Dalmally Road, and Christopher's grandmother had sharp ears. He had suspected on more than one occasion that she had lingered and lurked outside the bedroom door when Nick had been there, trying to catch them out in some unspeakable activity. Up in the attics at Marden, Nick had what virtually amounted to his own private suite. The neighbours lived too far away to be bothered by noise, and the attic stairs creaked underfoot, thus giving warning of any approaching busybodies. In fact no one in the

Sheringham household appeared to take the least bit of interest in any of the others' affairs. He couldn't remember, Nick said, when his mother had last been up to the attics.

This Saturday, as on many another Saturday, they had the entire house to themselves. Christopher didn't ask where the rest of the family were. Gerald, most likely, would be up in town, the au pair out with her boyfriend. Susan Sheringham would be at the golf club, her husband could be anywhere – anywhere *except* the golf club. The Sheringhams never did things together if it could possibly be avoided.

'What do you want to hear first?' said Nick. 'Let me play the Liszt. It's incredible stuff . . . some of the last he wrote. You just listen!'

In his mature years, Franz Liszt, after a lifetime of womanising, had renounced all things worldly and had turned to the Church. They sat for a while, when the record had finished, speculating what would make a man do such a thing; the conversation led back, inevitably, to what they had been talking about earlier in the week, before Pat MacMaster with his inane burbling had interrupted them.

'I'm still thinking about it,' said Nick. 'I can't make up my mind.'

'You don't think it's something they'd discuss together?'

'I don't think Guy would ever be swayed by any arguments other than his own.'

'But surely he'd at least talk about it? If he were having problems –'

'It's possible.'

'I mean, he wouldn't just lay it on him out of the blue? *I'm turning my back on everything we ever planned together?'*

'No. No, of course he wouldn't. He wouldn't do that.'

'So –'

'Maybe one evening when he got back from being on tour –'

'When they were listening to music –'

Nick unfolded himself from the floor, which was their habitual sitting place. Going over to the stereo he removed the Liszt and replaced it with something Christopher recognized at once as Mahler's Second: the *Resurrection*. Guy had played the *Resurrection* to Oliver in his rooms at Oxford, the first night they had met. Oliver always knew, now, that if Guy put that particular piece on the record player it meant, *This is serious: something we have to discuss.*

'Something –' Guy sat down, cross-legged, on the floor – 'that I have to talk to you about ... I don't know how you're going to take it. The fact is, I'm – I'm seriously considering entering the priesthood.'

They spent the rest of the evening being Guy and Oliver, agonizing over the decision which Guy felt called upon to make. By the time the last movement of the *Resurrection* had sunk to its glorious close, over eighty minutes later, Oliver had manoeuvred himself into the position of being a lapsed rather than a practising Catholic, whilst Guy had struggled to the painful conclusion that possibly, after all, the priesthood was not for him. Not only was the conclusion a painful one – Guy confessed he had long hankered after the religious way of life – but it had been painfully arrived at, via a long process of suffering and soul-searching, highly satisfactory to both parties.

It was Guy who got up to switch off the record player: Nick who turned to look at Oliver.

'Do you want to take the Liszt back with you to hear at your place?'

'Good idea,' said Christopher.

They were simply actors, playing roles; that was all it was. Creative people did that sort of thing. You only had to look at the Brontës – look at Charlotte with her romantic fantasy figure, the big bad bold Zamorna: he of the 'intensely black hair, curled luxuriantly'. If Charlotte had had a grandmother, she would probably have been told that she was unnatural. But Charlotte had turned into Currer Bell who had written *Jane Eyre*; and Zamorna, all along, had been but a dress rehearsal for Mr Rochester. That was the way that writers operated. The way they exercised their creative imagination. There was nothing unnatural about it. It was necessary to develop their craft. One day when Christopher was famous – when he had won the Booker, or maybe the Whitbread – he would reveal to the world that his adolescence had been blighted by the voice of his grandmother, perpetually claiming him to be unnatural. He would be able to laugh at it then.

On Monday morning a message came through for Nick, via the secretariat: *The Headmaster would like to see you during mid-morning break*. Christopher was left on his own, at the mercy of the common room. The library was a non-starter, having been taken over for a lecture by some visiting pomposity: the Field was awash with the autumn monsoon. He lurked for a while in the main corridor, waiting for Nick to emerge, wondering what had caused him to be summoned to the Presence, but after one of the secretaries had passed and repassed him, and then passed yet again, stalking the school on affairs of state, he began to feel conspicuous and so moved on. Everywhere he attempted to secrete himself people seemed to be in occupation – holding meetings, having seminars, playing musical instruments. He was forced back, in the end, to the common room.

Screaming Virago were pumping out the decibels. He had heard them often enough, by now, to recognize the sound they made. Striving to be sociable, to show himself not completely cut off from the ordinary things of life, he said casually to Harry Morgan, 'Ever listen to Rik Harper?'

'Rik Harper?' Morgan looked at him as if he were something alien that had just crawled out of a time capsule. 'He's dead.'

Christopher said, '*Dead?*'

'D–e–d. Dead. Dead and buried. *Gone.*'

'When did that happen?' It must have been recent. The way Sarah had been talking –

'Months ago. Where have you been living? Hole in the ground?'

Morgan turned away, with his usual display of contempt. Christopher felt his cheeks begin to burn. Even when you tried to communicate on their level they wouldn't come halfway to meet you. Tony Forbes, standing nearby, obviously feeling sorry for him, said: 'He just means he's not in the charts any more. That's all.'

He didn't see Nick to talk to until the lunch break. After the usual cafeteria meal of recycled compost, covered in the brown sludge which passed for gravy, they left the building and made their way across to Holt Wood, to their favourite spot beneath a yew tree, where all but the worst of downpours failed to penetrate. Now that they were officially young men, as opposed to young monsters, no longer encased in purple uniform and liable to bring shame on the school, they were permitted during lunch breaks to wander abroad and mingle with the rest of humanity, but since the College was situated at the extreme top of Holt Hill, with only the Sandrock Pub (strictly out of bounds even for third-year sixth) and a petrol station within reach, most people didn't bother. In spring and summertime a few boys might be seen, pursuing their nefarious activities in the wood – smoking, shagging, carving holes in the trees – but in winter, for the most part, they had the place to themselves.

Christopher was anxious to know what had gone on in the Presence. 'What did Bogey want?'

'Nothing much.' Nick seemed disinclined to enter into any details. 'Just a general jaw. Did you manage to hear that Liszt yet? What did you think of it? Stupendous, isn't it?'

It wasn't until they had gone back into school, until, in fact, they were on the brink of a double period of English, that he said, 'By the way, he twisted my arm . . . I've had to say I'll do a number for them.'

'For the revue?'

'Just the one. They're not roping me in for any more.'

It was surprising enough – more than surprising: disconcerting, almost – that he should have agreed even that much. Nick was not the sort to have his arm twisted. In all their time at Astley, Christopher had never known him to capitulate. He had been adamant on Saturday evening, as they sat together in his attic domain, that no way was he allowing the demands of school to encroach upon his private life.

'I know what it would be . . . rehearsals in the evening, rehearsals during the lunch break, rehearsals at the weekend . . . could you come in on Saturday morning? Could you manage the odd Sunday? No, thank you! I have other things to do.'

He couldn't understand, now, what had made him climb down. It wasn't like Nick; it was totally out of character. He wanted to ask him, 'How come?', but Nick had timed it too well: they had no chance to talk either then, or, as it so happened, afterwards. Afterwards, presumably, was purely fortuitous – not even Nick could have arranged for their paths, on the way out of the building, to cross with that of Dr Bogaerts on his way in. Christopher had the feeling, however, that with or without headmasterly intervention Nick would have found some means of avoiding the subject.

'Seymour!' Dr Bogaerts hailed him with clawlike hand. 'Finished for the day? I wonder if I could just have a – mm – word with you?'

He felt the pressure of Nick's elbow in his ribs.

'See you anon,' murmured Nick.

Christopher turned and trailed silently in the wake of the Headmaster, up the wide staircase which led to the front hall and the secretariat. The outer office was deserted, but in the inner sanctum Mrs Barley was still at her post. She looked concerned as she saw Dr Bogaerts walk through with Christopher at his heels.

'You haven't forgotten, Headmaster? You have a parent coming at four o'clock?'

'Ah –' Dr Bogaerts stopped for a moment in his tracks. He was a tall, vague man, of thrifty and secretive habits. He probably had forgotten. Christopher braced himself, hopefully. 'Mm . . . yes –'

'It's now ten-to,' said Mrs Barley.

'Ten to four ... yes. Well — that shouldn't present us with any — ah — problems. I think we can ... mm ... yes. Come on in, Seymour! Come along in! I shan't — mm — detain you for very long. Just a brief word. Ten minutes, Mrs Barley. That is all we shall be.'

They walked through into the study. Dr Bogaerts took up his favourite position in his swivel chair, reclining gracefully with legs crossed, one hand dangling into space, the other toying with a silver paperknife.

'Take a seat, Seymour.' He motioned, graciously, with the paperknife. 'Make yourself — mm — comfortable.'

There were two chairs on offer: one a recliner, the other an upright. Christopher perched on the edge of the upright, wondering as he did so which one Nick had chosen.

'I have been meaning —' The Headmaster swivelled, mesmerically, waving his paperknife — 'meaning for some time to have a — mm — talk with you. I had hoped, once you were in the sixth form, with all its attendant freedoms and — mm — responsibilities, I had hoped that you might moderate your — ah — behaviour — behaviour — of your own accord. Such, however, seems not to have occurred; and I must say to you, Seymour, must say quite frankly, that I am more than a little perturbed by your — ah — mm ... attitude. In general. Does this surprise you, Seymour?'

Christopher said, 'I suppose it does a bit, sir.'

'Mm. I am surprised that it surprises you. You're an intelligent boy. Nick Sheringham is another intelligent boy. He, too, professed himself surprised. I cannot believe, cannot bring myself to believe, that two such intelligent boys can have come as far as the sixth form and failed to recognize that their behaviour is a cause

73

of concern. To tell you the truth, Seymour, you and Sheringham between you are a source of very grave anxiety to me. It has been forced upon my notice over the past few terms that you are isolating yourselves in a manner totally unacceptable.'

Christopher sat, without saying anything. The Headmaster suddenly lunged forward and pointed with his paperknife in one swift movement.

'Tell me something! Why is it that neither of you ever seems willing to participate in any in-school activities?'

Christopher licked his lips. He had always known it would cause comment, one of these days. They could never be content just to leave you alone to do your own thing. He said, 'We're not really joining sort of people.'

How often had he had this conversation with his grandmother? *It's not natural, boy of your age . . .*

'It's not that we're anti-social. It's just that − well, the sort of things that interest us −' writing; listening to music; being Guy and Oliver − 'they're not really the sort of things that you can do in bunches.'

The Headmaster brushed this aside with an impatient wave of the paperknife.

'It's wrong. All wrong! You're not giving of your best to the school. You're taking everything, and offering nothing in return. If you were boys who had nothing to offer − but you're not! That's the tragedy of it. Nick Sheringham, for example. I'm given to understand he's a singularly gifted musician . . . why has the school never heard of this? Why has he never come forward? Never offered us his talents? And you, Seymour! What has become of all the promise you once showed? When I look back −' The Headmaster swung forward again to

74

consult a single sheet of paper contained within a clear plastic folder – 'when I look back I see that in each of your first four years you made valuable contributions to the school magazine. In your third and fourth years I see honourable mentions of your name in connexion with the Junior Hockey Shield – "one of the team's top scorers". After that –' the Headmaster flipped the folder shut with a flamboyant movement of the fingers – 'nothing! Nothing at all! So where has it all gone, Seymour? What has happened? Why, for instance, let me put it to you, are you not serving on the editorial board of the magazine? *That* is a contribution you could very easily make.'

If anyone ever invited him. But nobody would; not now.

'And what of hockey? A game, yes; a mere game. Of no great account in the overall scheme of things. But where the good of the school is concerned ... I am told the hockey team is desperate for players. Where are you, in their hour of need? I can scarcely believe the skills of yester-year have so suddenly departed.'

Not his hockey-playing skills, perhaps; only his social skills. If he had ever had any. He could still remember, in humiliating detail, the torture of team get-togethers, of team teas, of team coach journeys to and from, everyone laughing, shouting, creating mayhem, Harry Morgan and Randy Robson, the two roaring boys, always the centre of every hubbub, and himself, on the fringes, relegated to the outer darkness. Even when he had been invited to the party he had never found a way of joining in. If Nick had been there – but Nick wouldn't play hockey. He wouldn't play cricket. Wouldn't put his hands at risk. Nick didn't care what other people thought.

'Well?' cried the Headmaster. 'I await enlightenment!'

Stiffly, he mumbled: 'I don't believe in competitive sports.'

'Not good enough! Not good enough! That is mere rationalization! Do you not feel any pride, Seymour, in being a pupil at this school? No pride at all? Can it be that you are totally deaf to the claims of public duty? That you feel no sense of obligation? We open our doors to you, and how do you reward us? By taking all and giving nothing! I speak to the staff and am told that yes, Seymour and Sheringham are two of our high-flyers. Oxbridge material. And that is gratifying! I make no bones about it. But when I ask as to your *social* prowess – then, I fear, it becomes a totally different story. Different and – I have to say it – unedifying. Not one member of staff, when questioned, has said that he or she would care to place any reliance on your – mm – co-operation or loyalty. We have *your* interests at heart – but do you, I wonder, have ours? I have to doubt it, Seymour! On all the evidence, I have to doubt it. I give you a small but important example: last term. Open Day. Duchess of Gloucester.'

The Headmaster swelled forward with a certain urgency as his lips let drop the name.

'The Duchess of Gloucester! Our royal patron, Seymour –' the swivel chair, momentarily unbalanced, set off on a slow revolution. 'Her Royal Highness, who was gracious enough to attend on that day, despite all the manifold calls upon her time . . . *she* does not shirk her public duties!' The Headmaster put out a hand and caught at the edge of the desk to steady himself. 'But where were you, I wonder, upon that occasion?'

Christopher had been up in town with Nick. They had gone on a tour of second-hand bookshops. It had been their right: attendance at Open Day was not compulsory.

'These things get noticed, you see. They draw attention to you – in a manner which is not to your advantage. Do not forget that admission to a university depends not solely upon academic achievement but upon social qualities as well. What am I to write, if called upon for a testimonial? I put it to you, Seymour, what am I to write? Make me one suggestion!'

The words came to him, *He did not succumb to blackmail.* He remained silent.

The Headmaster plied his paperknife. To and fro, to and fro . . .

'I sometimes wonder,' he said, 'I do sometimes wonder, whether you and Sheringham are perhaps seeing rather too much of each other? Becoming a trifle too – mm – dependent on each other? I'm only saying this for your own good, you know. I'm not getting at you. I have no wish to destroy your individuality. Heaven forbid we should ever start turning out boys on a conveyor belt! But I would ask you, Seymour, to think over what I have said. Apply your mind to it as you would to an essay, or a difficult piece of translation. Approach it as a problem to be solved by the application of logic. Needless to say –' he reached out a languid hand as the intercom buzzed – 'I am always here should you wish to speak to me. I should like to think you would find me not unsympathetic. – Yes, Mrs Barley. We're finished now. – Very well, Seymour. Off you go! Bear in mind what we have spoken of.'

His one consolation was the thought that Nick had already been through it. But Nick had capitulated. That was worrying.

5

Postcards from Sarah continued to bombard him: *Just bought the latest Rik Harper album! Brill!!!*

With his new-found knowledge, he could not resist the reply: *Has no one told you that Rik Harper is dead and buried?*

The response was sharp and immediate: *WHO SAYS?*

He wrote back: *I do.*

To which, very smartly, she retorted: *What do you know about anything?*

Which momentarily stumped him. It took him a day or so to think up a suitable come-back:

> *About Rik Harper not a jot,*
> *About Debussy quite a lot.*
> *Likewise Liszt and Gustav Mahler,*
> *Not to mention Edward Elgar.*
> *You should strive your tastes to widen –*
> *Try some Bach and Joseph Haydn.*

To which she had the nerve to reply: *WHO BACH & JOSEPH HAYDN? WHICH GROUPS?*

He was almost beginning to enjoy the correspondence (he was still working on a suitable riposte to this latest) when she sent a card which seemed to threaten his entire existence: *They think they may have found a house!! At last!!! Hawthorn Av – near you??? Mum coming over next week to have a look.*

'That'd be nice,' said his grandmother, thus proving beyond any doubt at all that she read the backs of his postcards. 'Helen and the family living nearby . . . I'd like that.'

Hawthorn Avenue wasn't exactly nearby, but still it was rather too close for comfort. He walked there, secretly, that afternoon, making a detour on his way back from school. It was at the opposite end of Holt Wood from Marden: down in the valley, where the wet Liberals lived. The houses were all Edwardian or late Victorian, detached, red-brick, most of them still in family occupation. Outside number 52 there was a FOR SALE board. He hurried past it, pretending not to look, then crossed the road and walked back rather more slowly, to have another look. It was just the sort of house where he could imagine the Sandersons: large, sprawling, double-fronted. Unless it was actually falling apart with dry rot, it seemed dismally certain that they would take it.

A string of jubilant cards from Sarah confirmed his fears.

They've made an offer on Hawthorn Av!

Offer accepted!!!

We are coming up end of term to see about schools!!!!!!

This last was particularly alarming: it meant he was going to have to meet Glenn. There was simply no way he could see of avoiding it. The one comfort he clung to was that even if the moron actually managed to make it to Astley they were not very likely to be in the same form. Christopher was Arts, Glenn, almost certainly, would be General Sciences. But even that was of minor comfort. The sixth was not so large that Glenn could fail to notice Christopher's almost total isolation. It would get back to his parents, get back to Sarah. He specially didn't like the thought of Sarah knowing.

One evening, to his horror, he was called to the telephone and there she was at the other end of the line, all giggling and bubbly. She didn't realize he was mad and unnatural and didn't know what to say. Fortunately, with Sarah, it didn't really matter: she said it all for him.

'We're coming over next weekend, Glenn's got to go and see this Headmaster of yours, *old Bogey.*'

She knew from Christopher that he was called old Bogey. She had asked him, on a postcard, *What name of your headmaster? What like? Glenn wants know worst.*

'Dad's going with him, and Mum's coming with me, I've got to go to this place called Percy's . . . have you heard of it? The Lady *Perceval* School? Sounds a bit off, if you ask me. Anyway, we're going there and then we're meeting Dad and Glenn and we're going to have some lunch and just a minute, I think Mum wants something, she's hovering, making gestures – I'm still talking to Christopher! I've only just started. I *know* about the phone bills, but it's after 6 p.m. . . . well, I won't be long. I just want to ask him something. I just wanted to ask you, you know this revue that Rik Harper's in? The one you told me about, where he's playing the piano? Well, I was telling them about it and Mum said why didn't we all go, as we're going to be here, and it's on the Saturday, and we could drive back to Salisbury afterwards, so she said to ask you – I'm only asking him what you told me to ask him! – to ask you whether you can get tickets and if you can, could you get some for us, and if you let us know how much they are we'll send you the money. Is that OK? And if your gran's there, could you tell her Mum's here and she'd like a word with her?'

He handed over, with relief, to his grandmother. He wondered if he could get away with saying there were no more tickets left for the end-of-term revue. He and Nick never went to school functions. They never went anywhere near school out of official school hours; not if it could possibly be avoided. Nick had said he didn't see why Christopher should have to suffer the waste of a Saturday evening just because he was having to. He would have gone, had Nick wanted him to; but he had the impression Nick would genuinely rather he didn't. He suspected, though couldn't be certain, since Nick was not a person who ever opened up on the subject of his own feelings, that there might be an element of shame attached – shame at having allowed himself to be blackmailed. They had never discussed it, just as they had never discussed what music Nick was going to play. Every now and again he would go off for a rehearsal, leaving Christopher to mooch by himself about the Field, or skulk behind a barrier of books in the library; but their tacit agreement was that it should not be talked about.

He might have known, now the Sandersons were involved, that matters would immediately become complicated. They were that sort of family.

'What's all this about an end-of-term show?' It was

the first thing his grandmother said, as she came back from the telephone. He ought never to have mentioned it to Sarah. He couldn't think why he had, except that it had been something to write to her about. 'Why haven't your mother and I been invited? Never occurs to you, I suppose, that we might occasionally like to be part of what's going on?'

'I didn't think you'd be interested,' he said. 'It's a revue.'

'I like revues,' said Louise.

'So do I,' said his grandmother.

'The thing is, it's a bit late ... I expect all the tickets have probably been sold.'

'Nonsense! You tell them who they're for. They'll have a few tucked away.'

He tried forgetting about it, but she wouldn't let him. The minute he got in from school it was, 'Did you get those tickets for us?' And next morning, as he left: 'You just remember ... you get those tickets.' She wore him down in the end. He said apologetically to Nick: 'We've got to come to this cruddy revue.'

'Don't blame me,' said Nick. 'It wasn't my idea.'

He felt embarrassed, when the time came, walking into school with Louise and his grandmother and the whole tribe of Sandersons. People didn't expect to see him or Nick at public functions. He lived in dread of someone saying 'Fancy seeing you here!' but no one did. No one took the least bit of notice of him; which was, in its way, almost as bad. It could hardly escape the attention of the Sandersons that he was a social leper.

Sarah, who insisted on sitting next to him, kept whispering to him, pointing people out, asking him who they were, wanting to know whether they were in his class, whether they were friends of his. Once she giggled and said, 'Look, there's that boy with the hands!' The boy with the hands was Derek Siegenberg. He still couldn't see what was supposed to be wrong with them.

He found himself feeling not quite so awkward with her as he had before. It was a pity she looked so absurdly young. He had discovered that she was in fact only nine months younger than he was, but the extreme smoothness and roundness of her face made her look about twelve. No one was very likely to take her for his girlfriend. He had noticed Tony Forbes glancing speculatively at her once or twice, obviously trying to assess the relationship, not quite knowing what to make of it.

Glenn, a tall, surly youth with a crop of yellow-headed pimples, seemed no more disposed to talk to Christopher than Christopher was to talk to him. It had been Louise who asked him how his interview with the Headmaster had gone. Glenn had said, 'OK.'

'So you'll be starting next term?' had said Louise, all bright and sunny, doing her best.

Glenn had shrugged a shoulder. 'I guess.'

'That's good,' had said Louise, 'isn't it?'

'Hnh,' had said Glenn.

He only ever appeared to speak in grunts and monosyllables. He was a natural for the Harry Morgan-Andy Robson set-up.

The revue, it had to be said, was nowhere near as cruddy as he had thought it was going to be. Parts of it were almost quite amusing – Harry Morgan, on the mediaeval spoons – though he could have made a far better job of some of the sketches. *If* anybody had thought to ask him. They knew he could write, he had persistently come top of every English exam he had ever taken. He hadn't tried to hide it, like Nick and his music. But Nick had social connexions: Christopher didn't. And anybody could write, everyone knew that. 'We all have a book inside us,' they said, *pour encourager* the Glenns of this world. We couldn't all play the piano.

Nick's piano-playing stopped the show. He did one of the big bravura pieces, *Czardas Macabre*, from the double album of Liszt which they had bought at Weedon's. Christopher sat stunned, as the great rolling chords came thundering across the hall. He hadn't known that Nick could play like that. It shook him, rather. He wasn't sure what he had been expecting. Something polite by Mozart? A Beethoven bagatelle? He had taken technical expertise for granted – Nick was a perfectionist: he would not be Nick if he had performed incompetently – but nothing on such a scale as this.

The audience, which had a tendency to be highbrow (he discounted people such as his grandmother) recognized quality when they heard it: mediaeval spoons might make them laugh, but this was for real. They showed their appreciation in a storm of applause almost as tumultuous as the music itself. Christopher joined in, but felt self-conscious; almost as if Nick, from his position on stage, could see him in the darkness of the auditorium, clapping along with the rest, and was cocking a cynical eyebrow. He had to translate himself into Oliver, and Nick into Guy – Oliver attending one of Guy's concerts – before he could lose the feeling. Sarah, leaning towards him so that her hair brushed his cheek, whispered, 'He *does* look like Rik Harper!'

Afterwards they walked back with the Sandersons to the car park. Mel Sanderson said, 'Well! That young man can certainly tickle the ivories.'

Helen Sanderson groaned.

84

'That's Christopher's friend,' said Sarah. 'Rik,' she said; and she dug Christopher in the ribs and giggled.

'Nick,' said Louise. 'I must admit, he was very good.'

She at least could be generous. It was more than his grandmother could.

'Tuneless, I'd call it. Nothing but a load of noise. And not really in keeping.'

Sarah looked at Christopher and pulled a face. Almost involuntarily, he pulled one back. She giggled and said, 'See you at Christmas!'

'What did she mean?' said Christopher, as the Sandersons' car pulled away.

'What she said,' said his grandmother.

Louise, sounding nervous, said: 'We've all been invited down to Salisbury for the Christmas period. I know you usually see Nick, but –'

'Nick's not going to be here,' he said.

'Oh.' Louise relaxed, visibly. 'That's all right, then.'

It wasn't all right; he still wouldn't choose to go to Salisbury – the whole of Christmas in the company of that monosyllabic moron, Glenn? – but with Nick away there was no point in putting up a fight.

'Where is he going?' said Louise, happy now that there was no competition. 'Anywhere exciting?'

'He's going to Switzerland.'

His grandmother sniffed. 'Nice if you can get it.'

Louise, trying hard – there were times, he could tell, when she really felt bad about not liking Nick – said, 'Of course, his grandmother hasn't been too well, has she? Is she any better now?'

'She had a heart attack. But she's back at home.'

'Heart attack! At her age.' His grandmother pounced, eagerly. She was always insanely exultant over other people's ailments. 'How old is she, anyway?'

He shrugged. 'No idea.'

Nick never talked about his grandmother. He spent every summer with her, but he never talked about her. (Like he spent every evening playing the piano and had never talked about that, either.)

'Must be about my age, I suppose. Drinks too much, probably. Smokes too much. Too much high living. Money isn't everything in this life, you mark my words.'

'So who are these relatives,' said Nick, 'anyway?'

'Something to do with my grandmother . . . her niece, or something.'

'Who? The girl?'

'No, her mother.'

'So what relation does that make her to you? Second cousin?'

'Dunno.' He wasn't really terribly interested in what relation Helen Sanderson was to him. He couldn't understand why Nick had to keep on about it. He had only mentioned the Sandersons because he had thought he might like to know that they had appreciated his piano-playing. With intent to amuse he had also thrown in the information that Sarah habitually referred to him as Rik Harper; and by way of general grievance had further added that he was being hauled down to Salisbury for Christmas and that after Christmas the Sandersons were moving up to Holt Wood, 'and that moron is coming to Astley.'

Nick had appeared not to care one way or another what anyone thought of his piano-playing, nor had he picked up on the Rik Harper reference. What puzzled him, what he couldn't understand, was why anyone in their right mind should want to come to Holt Wood.

He kept returning to it. Why Holt Wood? What was the attraction?

'My grandmother sold them the idea. She thought it'd be nice and cosy to have family here.'

'I hope they're not going to expect you to drag round with them.'

He shook his head. 'We've got nothing in common. The guy's an idiot.'

'What about the girl?'

'Sarah? She's just a kid. You don't have to worry about her.'

'I'm not worried. Who said I was worried?'

'Well ... going on about it. It's bad enough I have to spend Christmas with them.'

'You wait till they're living on the doorstep,' said Nick.

*

Christopher could not remember ever having had access to so much free drink before. Beer, wine, spirits, lager ... they floated giddily in front of his eyes like so many pink elephants.

'Once a year,' said Mel Sanderson. 'Just once a year. We reckon it doesn't do too much harm.'

At Marden there were always unlimited supplies, but Nick, unlike the rest of his family, was a strict teetotaller. In Dalmally Road the most that ever appeared, even just once a year, was a bottle of what his grandmother called 'table wine'.

He had a faint, happy, totally untroubled feeling that faced with such a plethora of choice he had taken too many samples from too many bottles. He wondered if perhaps he might be described as being slightly the worse for wear. He tried to hold on to the coherent

87

thought that it was a new and valid experience. Not necessarily one to be repeated, but one to be savoured and stored up for future use.

A thought came to him, meandering vaguely through the alcoholic euphoria . . . suppose Oliver were to go through a phase of excessive drinking? So much so that he was in danger of becoming dependent on it? He pictured Oliver wrestling with the problem, just as Guy had had to wrestle with his conscience over whether or not to enter the priesthood. The idea appealed. He set it to one side to be dwelt upon later in the privacy of bed.

A slight movement at his side caused him, with extreme gingerness, to raise his head. Sarah's round moon face beamed and bobbed through an alcoholic haze

'This is fun,' she said, 'isn't it?'

She was curled up next to him, nose to tail, on an old sagging sofa in what he supposed, dimly, to be some kind of junk room. He had no very clear memory of how they had arrived there. They appeared to be on their own; at any rate, peering through the fog he could not make out anyone else.

'What do you usually do at Christmas?' She snuggled closer, burrowing up to him like a small animal. He wondered if she, too, was suffering from excessive consumption or whether, for her, this was quite normal behaviour. 'Mm?' She poked her fringe to one side, staring earnestly up. 'What d'you ordinarily do?'

He concentrated. 'Not a lot.'

'Don't you see Nick?'

'Not necessarily.' That was a lie: he and Nick always met up at Christmas. They had done so for years.

'Your grandmother said you did. She said –' Sarah did an uncanny imitation of his grandmother's voice, cracked and crotchety – ' "Oh, we never have the pleasure of *his* company. Too busy doing his own thing round at his boyfriend's." '

In the dim light (he hoped it really was dim, and not just his alcoholic perception of it) he felt his cheeks fire up. Sarah giggled.

'They're awful,' she said, 'aren't they? Grand-mothers?'

'Yours seems OK.'

'That's only 'cause we don't usually live with her. Mum says it's a mistake for different generations to live together. She says it's OK if you can afford a proper granny flat, but not if you're all cooped up together . . . I think if we were going to stay here much longer,' said Sarah, 'Mum and Gran would probably fall out. She keeps on about me and Glenn . . . about our "Australian manners".'

'What –' He strove to speak lucidly, but his tongue seemed to have swollen to gigantic proportions. It was like a huge jellyfish in his mouth. 'What are Australian manners?'

'Being too *forward*. Being *brash*. She says, "Sarah, you're so *brash*. And that *accent* –" '

He said, 'You do have a slight Australian accent.'

'So what? It's better than being all stuffy and English and upper crust.'

He hadn't said that it wasn't. He hadn't been criti-cising; just stating a fact.

'Whah, whah, whah,' said Sarah. 'I can't *stand* that. They'd better not try making me speak like it . . . I s'pose they all do, at that place you go to?'

89

They didn't all. He didn't – but he was only schol-arship. That probably didn't count.

'What about Nickelarse? Does he?'

He tried to hear Nick's voice, but the fumes from the various bottles he had sampled were making strange ringing noises in his head.

'Does he?' said Sarah.

'I dunno. Never thought about it.'

'I bet he does,' said Sarah. 'Living in that great enormous place.' She suddenly giggled again and let her head fall on to his shoulder. 'I think I'm squiffy!'

Squiffy, he thought. What a strange word. Squiffy. Where could she have got it from?

''Zat Aus'trane?' he said.

'What?'

'S-quiffy.'

'No. It's what my gran says. When my granddad has one too many ... "William," she says, "you're squiffy." '

She wriggled herself round and hooked an arm about him. He felt a curious tingling up and down his vertebrae, like a hidden hand playing on a xylophone. He wondered if this was foreplay and if so at what stage it started to get out of hand.

'Has Nickelarse got a girlfriend?' she said.

He didn't like her asking all these questions about Nick. It seemed a betrayal to talk about him with Sarah, behind his back.

'*Has* he?'

'No.'

'Why not?'

'He hasn't got time for them. He's very hardworking.'

'Like you. You're very hardworking. Your grand-mother says so. "*Never has his nose out of a book ...*"

You know that music he played? At the end-of-term thingie? I've bought it. It's the only classical record I've got. Glenn thinks I'm mad. I've been playing it over and over; just that one piece. I'm almost getting to know it. It's a bit weird, but I quite like it. Does he always play that sort of stuff?'

'He doesn't usually play at all, in public.'

'Why not?'

Why not, why not? Why this, why that?

'Music means a lot to him. He likes to keep it private.'

'He sounds like a very private sort of person.'

He grunted. His right arm, squashed beneath Sarah, was beginning to get pins and needles, but he didn't like to move it in case she took it as a mark of protest. It wasn't a mark of protest; he enjoyed the feel of her body pressed up against him, even if his right arm was getting pins and needles. Tendrils of ideas relating to Oliver kept creeping into his befuddled mind. He had to keep pushing them back. Now was not the time for exploring them. Later, when he could do so at leisure –

Sarah gave a small sigh and nuzzled her face into his sweater. Tentatively – very tentatively – he rescued his right arm and slid it round her. She mumbled something which sounded like, 'Doosma bough that ole wood.'

'Doosma bough that,' she said.

'Yeah.' He nodded, encouragingly; and then, emboldened, closed his other arm about her. It was only when she had fallen asleep, making tiny whirring snores which kept blowing her fringe up and down, that he finally managed to translate what she had said: *We'll have to do something about that when we come to Holt Wood . . .*

He was too pleasantly woozy at the time to be alarmed.

*

He woke up in his own bed – or rather, Glenn's bed: Glenn was sleeping in his sleeping-bag on the floor – at some late hour the next morning. He had been dreaming that he had a large woolly sheepdog sitting on his tongue, and upon investigation with a fingernail he found it to be thickly coated with a bright yellow substance, faintly furry in nature. A bulldozer was moving mountains of earth from one part of his head to another, and someone was knocking at the bedroom door. It must have been the knocking which had woken him.

Before he could mobilize his tongue sufficiently to say 'Come in', the door had opened and Sarah, swathed in a red woolly bathrobe, was padding into the room.

'Hi,' she said.

'Hi.' He propped himself on an elbow and balanced, uncertainly. Glenn's sleeping-bag, he noticed, had disappeared.

'How ya feeling?' She surveyed him, owlishly, through the spiky strands of a plastered-down fringe. 'I've bin sick three times already. And more to come. I can feel it, just here –' her hands pressed into the pit of her stomach. 'Just waiting to bubble up . . . that is the first and last time I am ever going to touch alcohol. By the bones of all the martyrs, alcohol shall never knowingly cross my lips again . . . the game, my friend, is not worth the candle. I thought when you told me about old Nickelarse being TT he was some kind of puritanical nut, but I am here to tell you –' she burped and put a hand to her mouth – 'I am here to tell you that he definitely knows what he's talking about.'

Christopher frowned. He had told her about Nick not drinking? He had no memory of doing so. He wondered uncomfortably what else he might have told her.

'I don't know whether I look as ghastly as I feel,' she said. 'Do you reckon you feel as ghastly as you look?'

'I feel –' he said it carefully, not sure what eruptions it might cause, down in the depths of his stomach – 'as if someone's bashing my brains with a ten-ton hammer.'

'Yeah.' She nodded, unwisely vigorous, and laid a hand on top of her head. 'Me, too. Mind you, it was fun while it lasted.'

He tried to grin, to signal agreement, but even that slight movement created inner turmoil. The bulldozers shifted another half hundredweight from the back of his head to the front: the hammer swung and pounded. He felt his stomach balloon upwards into his mouth. Sarah watched him, interested but sympathetic.

'You bin sick yet?'

'Glm.' He shook his head, very slowly and geriatrically.

'I expect you will be. One time when Glenn got plastered he threw up all over the back of the car . . . Dad was furious. Mum says everyone has to do it once and learn from their own experience. D'you think Nickelarse ever did?'

'Glm.' Nick had already learnt from the experience of his mother. He didn't need experience of his own.

'Well, anyway,' said Sarah, 'I'm going back to bed now. I thought I'd better just come and say goodbye to you before you go home.'

He had forgotten they were going home. They were supposed to be catching the twelve o'clock train. That meant Louise would be up here at any moment, rattling curtains and telling him to get out of bed.

'I'll see you in a week or two,' said Sarah. 'I'll write you before then. Oh, and hey –' she paused at the door – 'when you write back . . . I'm Sal, remember? I can't stand it when people put Sarah. OK?'

He mumbled, 'OK.'

In the train on the way back to Holt Wood, his grandmother teased him. (He assumed it was teasing. It was impossible to be certain, except that she didn't sound quite as malicious as she usually did.)

'Well!' she said. 'I'm surprised we're able to put one foot in front of the other, state we were in last night.'

She sounded almost as if she approved of the state he had been in; as if in some muddled kind of way it proved his manhood. Big Man, Him get Fighting Drunk . . . It was one of the few things he had ever done – perhaps that and passing the scholarship to Astley were in fact the *only* things he had ever done – which had sent him up rather than down in her esteem. Well, she needn't think he was going out on a bender every week just to keep her happy. He knew some of the guys did, Morgan and Robson were forever boasting of their alcoholic exploits, not that he believed more than a quarter of it; but who wanted to end up like those two brain-damaged robots?

'Well away,' said his grandmother. 'You and young Sally, carrying on up there . . . looks like you've found yourself a sweetheart.'

Louise giggled; she sounded almost like Sarah. 'Mum! You're way out of date. They don't have *sweet*hearts, these days.'

'So what do they have then? Dolly birds?'

'Just girlfriends, I think.'

94

She looked at him, hopefully, wanting him to confirm it. He could imagine her, at work in the Merrie Kettle, telling the women she worked with, 'Christopher's found himself a girlfriend at last.' It would be nice for her, he could see that. She would like to be able to tell the girls – she always called them girls, even though they were middle-aged – about him and Sarah in the junk room. 'There they were, all cuddled up together.' It would raise her status, having a son who was normal and got a bit tiddly and cuddled with girls, rather than one who did nothing but sulk upstairs in his room listening to Shostakovitch.

'She's a nice little thing,' said Louise.

'Certainly made a beeline for Mr Clever Clogs here . . . I don't know what she sees in him, I'm sure. He's obviously got something I don't know about. Mind you –' his grandmother humped her handbag further on to her lap, holding it there with plump bespeckled fingers – 'there's one person who's not going to be best pleased about it, and that's You Know Who . . . young master Nicholas isn't going to like it, is he? Push his nose properly out of joint. About time, too. Had things his own way for far too long, that young gentleman.'

She nodded, triumphant, across the carriage at Christopher. 'Money can't buy everything, as I've said before. Just one of the lessons we all have to learn.'

6

The Sandersons had moved into Hawthorn Avenue in the middle of January. At the end of January they had thrown a house-warming party. The house-warming had been on a Saturday and Christopher had been quite unable to wriggle out of it. Truth to tell, he had only half wanted to. He had protested more as a matter of principle than anything else – they weren't *his* relations: why drag him along? – secure in the knowledge that Louise would stand firm.

'Of course they're your relations! And of course you must come. Sarah will be expecting you.'

'Sal,' he'd said. 'She's told you, she likes to be called Sal.'

He had been apprehensive at seeing her again. It was his experience that what had worked once very rarely worked twice. He had learnt to accept it as one of the hard facts of life and had gone along fully prepared to be cold-shouldered, or, if not cold-shouldered, to find all over again, just as at the beginning, that he didn't know how to speak to her. They would stand in silence, mindlessly gorming at each other, and she would wonder what she had ever seen in him. If indeed she ever *had* seen anything in him. He had to keep reminding himself that they had both been drunk.

The house-warming had offered further opportunity for excess – 'Special occasion! You don't move house every day.' Left to himself, Christopher might well have succumbed, but Sarah had been there and had taken him to task.

'Eugh! Yuck! You're not turning into an alkie, are you? After *last* time? Put it down! It's horrible!'

He didn't mind her being forceful. He knew that he lacked willpower, for his grandmother had often told him so. And, besides, if it hadn't been for Sarah and her colonial brashness – 'That's what my gran calls it: your dreadful colonial *brashness*, Sarah' – they would never have moved beyond the stage of awkward small-talk. It had still been Sarah, even at the house-warming, who had made most of the conversation, but at least he had found himself able to respond without the constant need to weigh his every remark, calculating the effect it might have before he dared to utter it.

Two weeks after the house-warming, the Sandersons – with Sarah, minus Glenn – had come to Dalmally Road. They had come for afternoon tea and he and Sarah had gone for a walk. It had been Sarah's sugges-tion. They had walked through Holt Wood, where he had lived in dread of bumping into Nick and had instead bumped into Tony Forbes strolling hand in hand with a girl with red hair. He and Christopher had grinned, sheepishly, at each other. Sarah and the girl had waved and called out hello. Sarah had said afterwards, 'That was Debbie Mander. She's in my class.' She had only been at Percy's five minutes and already she seemed to be on intimate terms with the whole of her year.

She had asked him, on the way back to Dalmally

Road, if he felt like going to a disco that evening. He hadn't told her he was going round to Nick's. He had just said, 'A load of school work to catch up on.' She had pulled a face and said, 'On a *Saturday*?', but his reputation had already been well enough established: she accepted that he was the sort of brain-addled idiot who just might sit down and do a load of school work on a Saturday evening.

'Maybe over Easter?' she said.

'Yeah. Over Easter.'

By Easter, anything could have happened. He could have developed Huntingdon's chorea, Sarah could have given up on him, fundamentalist fanatics could have wiped out the world.

'I'll hold you to that!' she said.

One Sunday he took her to Chislehurst Caves. She had rung up to say that 'Glenn won't go with me and I'm scared to go by myself, someone told me they're really creepy.' They weren't really creepy, not with an official guide and the usual party of tourists, but he went anyway. He bought her a packet of home-made fudge and a model dinosaur from the gift shop, and when they got back to Hawthorn Avenue, Helen Sanderson insisted he come in for a cup of tea, which turned into a full-scale supper, at which the monosyllabic Glenn was present. Unlike Christopher, whose powers of conversation were limited mainly by embarrassment, Glenn seemed simply surly by nature.

'It's just a phase he's going through,' said Sarah, up in her room afterwards. 'Mum says it's normal adolescence and he'll grow out of it. *Maybe.* I wouldn't place too much reliance on it. Of course he's worse when someone like you is around . . . you make him feel inferior.'

'Me?' He was not fishing for compliments; his amazement was quite genuine. He was not actually sure that he believed it. Glenn, as he had predicted, had quickly teamed up with Harry Morgan and his mob. He must be very well aware by now of Christopher's total lack of standing in the school community. He must know that he was mad and unnatural. Why should Glenn feel inferior?

'No brain,' said Sarah. She tapped a finger to her forehead. 'Mum keeps telling him they'll be just as proud of a son who's a good motor mechanic as they would of one who got to Oxford and ended up with letters after his name, but he knows darn well she's only saying it to make him feel better . . . you don't know how lucky you are not having any pressures.'

Him? Not have pressures? She must be joking! His grandmother was a pressure in herself.

'How about Nick?' she said. She was forever asking him questions about Nick. 'Are his parents always getting on at him?'

'I'm not sure Nick's parents are properly aware of his existence.'

Her eyes grew big. 'You mean, he's adopted?'

'No, I mean they don't really take much notice of him.'

'Gee, I wouldn't like *that*!'

'I would,' he said.

'No, you wouldn't! That's just being flip. You'd hate it . . . it does very bad things to a person's psyche, to be ignored by their parents. Listen, you want to hear my classical record?'

'Why don't we hear some Rik Harper?' he said.

'Hey, that's right! Broaden your musical horizons!'

*

School broke for Easter. The world was still intact, he had not (so far as he knew) developed Huntingdon's or any other kind of chorea; Sarah was still around.

'But you don't have to come to the disco if you don't want to,' she said. She forked her fringe out of her eyes. 'Mum says I'm getting too bossy. I guess she could be right. What shall we do instead?'

It could have been difficult, but as luck would have it, within three days of term ending Nick had unexpectedly flown off to Switzerland to be with his grandmother. Last Easter, such a defection would have left him resentful and bereft; this Easter, it seemed almost like a reprieve.

He spent much of the holiday going round to Hawthorn Avenue to have his horizons broadened, not only musically but in other ways as a result. He had discovered, for example, that pop music, while not very good for actually listening to, was a natural accompaniment to what his grandmother always referred to as 'snogging'.

'There they go!' she'd say, whenever people moved into a clinch on the television screen. 'Snogging again!'

He had fantasized about it so often, without any real expectation of his fantasies ever acquiring substance, that even now he found it hard to believe it was actually happening – that he, Christopher Seymour, unnatural, batty, bananas Seymour, was behaving the same as everyone else: got himself a *girlfriend*. He tried saying it aloud within the confines of his bedroom: 'My girlfriend.' And then again, 'Sal . . . the girl I go out with.'

He spoke to imaginary interviewers, come to record an interview with him for radio or television, telling them his life history, describing his gradual rise to literary fame and fortune. He had been giving these interviews for years. It was a form of reassurance: *one day* ... The difference now was that Sal had entered the picture. Before, it had been Nick – Nick or Guy, depending on whether he was being Christopher-being -interviewed or Oliver. It varied, according to mood. Now he introduced Sarah – 'My first conquest.'

'Of course, there've been countless others since then; but I shall always –' a little worldly-wise smile played about his lips as he addressed his reflection in the dressing-table mirror – 'I shall always remember Sal with special affection.'

More than once, just lately, he had found himself having thoughts about Oliver which for the first time ever he knew he couldn't confide to Nick. When he had had to miss out on their usual Saturday evening session round at Marden in order to go to the house-warming in Hawthorn Avenue, Nick had as good as said 'I told you so.' In fact what he had said was, 'You see? It's starting.' Christopher had hotly denied it.

'Nothing's *starting*. This is just a one-off. People do this sort of thing when they move to new houses. It won't be happening again.'

As far as Nick was concerned, it hadn't – at any rate, not on a Saturday. Christopher hadn't told him about the walks in Holt Wood (they had gone for several more since that first one when they had bumped into Tony Forbes) nor about the expedition to the Caves. He certainly wouldn't be telling him about the evenings spent listening to Rik Harper. There was a line in a play called *Private Lives*, by Noël Coward, which he and Nick had seen last year at the theatre in Bromley. It came back to him, quite often: *Extraordinary how potent cheap music is.* Nick hadn't liked the play (he had dismissed it as facile: they had argued about it) and he wouldn't understand the incredible truth contained in the line. Impossible to imagine Nick listening to Rik Harper with his arm round a girl. For better or for worse, Nick seemed totally removed from the ordinary workaday concerns of life. Once Christopher had envied him; now he was not so sure.

The first Saturday of the summer term he went round, as usual, to Marden. Sarah was going to a rock concert with Glenn and a girl called Masha Kranz. She had said to him, in wistful tones, 'I suppose it's not really your scene?' He had agreed that it wasn't but couldn't help thinking about it as he trudged up the hill to Marden. It would at least have been a new experience. One ought to have new experiences.

Nick met him at the door. He was wearing his usual weekend gear of black sweater and black trousers – as opposed to his weekday gear of navy sweater and grey trousers. Nick always dressed in sombre colours. Christopher couldn't ever remember seeing him in anything bright, and he never wore jeans. Louise had asked him once, when he and Christopher had first become friends, 'Doesn't your mother worry about you tearing holes in those good trousers?' That was before she had learnt about Nick's mother.

'Come on up.' Nick started up the stairs ahead of him. 'That Elgar we got this morning is something else!'

'Which Elgar? The symphony, or –'

'No, the *Enigma*. Come and have a listen!'

He found it strangely difficult, that evening, to keep his attention from wandering. Perhaps if the music had been less familiar he might have found it somewhat easier, but he had known the *Enigma Variations* for years. There had once been a time when Nick had played them obsessively, over and over, until every bar, almost every note, was as well known to him as lines of poetry. Or maybe he was simply not in a mood for in-depth concentration. He kept thinking about Sarah, and about Guy and Oliver, exploring a whole new area of thought that was both strange and disturbing.

He glanced now and again at Nick, sitting with his eyes closed, listening to the music. He wondered if Nick had ever experienced these things: whether he, also, had hidden dreams he had not divulged to Christopher.

'What's the matter?' Nick spoke without opening his eyes. 'What do you keep shifting about for?'

'Sorry.'

Nick hated to be disturbed when he was listening to music. He rearranged himself into a more comfortable position and tried to keep still and silent and develop a thought about Oliver; though it struck him, guiltily, that by introducing his secret life into the private world he shared with Nick he was only making his betrayal the more complete.

'Listen.' It was Guy's hand which closed, with sudden urgency, over his knee. Nick wouldn't do a thing like that. He and Nick never touched each other. 'This is *Nimrod*.'

He knew it was *Nimrod*. He knew it as well as Nick – or as well as Guy. Nimrod, the great hunter; named for Elgar's friend, Jaeger. Der Jaeger, the hunter. First the strings, pianissimo; followed by woodwind and horns; then the broad main theme, like a river, slowly rolling in.

As the great Elgarian phrases sublimely arched and swelled, Guy's grip tightened on his knee. It was a demand for commitment: forbidding half-heartedness. Obediently he gave himself up to the music, as he had so many times before, letting it lift him and carry him, bearing him aloft on the heart-aching intensity of surging strings to the final shattering, soul-rending thunder of the climax.

There was silence. Slowly, Guy's grip relaxed. He uncrossed his legs, rose fluently to his feet, went across to the record player and lifted the arm before the next variation could begin.

'If ever there were music for dying to, that has to be it.'

Was it Guy who said it? Or was it Nick? He genuinely couldn't be certain.

'If I should die –' Flippantly, mock heroic, one hand to his breast, to break the tension, he declaimed their parody of Rupert Brooke – 'think only this of me: that there's some corner of a foreign field that is for ever fed by the daft dumb bones of some misguided English clod.'

The lines continued: *a clod whom England bore, misshaped, made unaware* – but Nick (Guy?) did not take it up. He said, 'If I should die, play *Nimrod* for me.'

It had to be Guy: Nick was not one to talk of dying. By all the unspoken rules of the game, he should now assume the mantle of Oliver. He found himself for once oddly reluctant to do so. He dipped his head, placing the soles of his feet together, striving to press his knees down to the floor as he had seen Sarah so effortlessly do.

'Let's hear something else,' he said. 'Something a bit less wrenching.' He quoted the idiot, MacMaster: 'How's about a bit of the old Debuss?'

'I don't feel like Debussy.' This time it was definitely

Guy. 'I feel like something tortured and soul-searing . . .
I shall play *Gerontius*.'

The Dream of Gerontius. Christopher pulled a face:
you couldn't get much more tortured and soul-searing
than that. He reminded himself that friendship exacted
its own dues; and settled down to an illicit dream of
Oliver in the throes of secret passion.

Three weeks into the summer term, Sarah started badgering him about parties.

'There's one next Saturday. Debbie Mander's giving
it. It'll be great! Her parents have this restaurant over
in Orpington and they're letting her use the banqueting
suite while it's closed for refurbishing. A whole banqueting suite! Can you imagine? A *banqueting* suite?'

He raised both eyebrows, to show he was impressed.
Even as he did so his brain was roaring into overdrive,
searching for excuses. He had known this was going to
happen one day.

'You ought to come,' said Sarah. 'You've never been
to a party with me.'

'No. I know. The thing is –' he clutched, feebly, at the
first straw that presented itself – 'it's a bit short notice.'

'A week?'

'Well – Saturday. It's – it's a bit –'

She stood, waiting. He clamped his fingers in his
hair. 'Saturdays are difficult,' he said.

'Why?' She was looking at him, curiously. 'You're
not a secretly religious Jew or something, are you?'

Improvising rapidly, he said: 'Nick and I are working
on this project together. Saturday's the only time we
really have for it.'

'What about Sunday? Couldn't you do it on a Sunday?'

'Nick's a Catholic. He goes to church on a Sunday.'
'*All day?*'

'Well – no, but –' He wasn't quite sure what Nick did for the rest of Sunday. Played the piano, probably. Whatever it was, he and Christopher didn't meet on Sundays. They never had, and Nick would think it odd if Christopher suddenly tried to change their habits after all this time. He would want to know why.

'Couldn't you take just *one* Saturday off?'

He muttered, 'It wouldn't be fair to Nick.'

'So why doesn't he come with us?'

'Nick?' Instinctively, he shied away from the idea. Nick was in one compartment of his life, Sarah in another. To admit of any communication between the two would be to invite disaster. It was something he knew, without even having to analyse the reasons why. 'Nick wouldn't want to come,' he said.

'Why not?'

'It's not his sort of thing. I told you, he's a very p–'

'A very private kind of person.' She chanted it, mockingly. For just a moment he was irritated.

'There's no law against being private, is there? They haven't made it an indictable offence yet? Or have they?'

'You don't have to get all aerated,' said Sarah.

'I'm not getting aerated, but I don't see why people can't just be left alone to do their own thing.' It was a battle he had been fighting all his life long – with his mother, with his grandmother, with Bogey, now with Sarah. Why couldn't people just leave people alone? 'If he wants to stay indoors and listen to music, I don't see why he shouldn't be allowed to. It's not doing anyone any harm, is it?'

'It is if it stops *you* doing things. It's not good to

be anti-social, you get all closed in on yourself. The human being is naturally gregarious.'

He wasn't at all sure that that was true. There were those, it seemed to him, who had a herd mentality, and those who didn't. 'Not everybody wants to go round in a mob,' he muttered.

'There's a difference between going round in a mob and just being normally sociable. People that don't get out lose the ability to communicate. You don't want to lose the ability to communicate, do you?'

He thought, I don't have to stand here and be lectured by a schoolgirl. Nick wouldn't. He'd put her in her place soon enough. If she wasn't careful she'd grow up like his grandmother. Nothing but nag.

'I'll tell you what,' she said. 'Suppose I organized a girl for him? There's plenty of kids in my year who wouldn't say no ... I mean, he's pretty nice-looking, and apart from being anti-social there's nothing actually wrong with him, is there? I mean, he's not the other way or anything?'

It was Glenn who'd put that suggestion in her head. He bet it was. He knew what they all thought, all those moronic bastards. He'd seen them whispering together, sniggering in their corners. He'd heard the silences which fell when he and Nick entered a room. That sort of thing didn't bother Nick; he probably didn't even notice it. But it did bother Christopher. He tried not to let it, he tried to remain cool and aloof, but he wasn't as well insulated as Nick.

'Hey, come on!' said Sarah. 'He's not, is he? I can't bear it! Every guy I ever look at, Glenn says, "He's a pouf" –'

He knew it had been Glenn. 'Some people,' he said, 'just have naturally perverted minds.'

'And how! My dear brother has a mind like a *sewer* ... do you know what he once tried telling me? He actually tried telling me that *Rik Harper* was a transvestite?'

'His idea of a joke,' said Christopher.

'I dunno. I sometimes think he really believes all this junk ... Anyway.' Sarah forked at her fringe. 'How about it? You want me to give it a go? There's a girl in our class, Angela Finch, she's into classical music. Bach and Beethoven and that. Shall I ask her if she'd like to meet him? I could, quite easily. If you think it would be a good idea.'

He thought it would be a lousy idea. If there was one thing Nick couldn't stand, it was people patronizing him.

'Sal –' Greatly daring, he put both his arms about her. She snuggled up to him, instantly. She was a very tactile sort of person. He still found physical contact, although exciting, not altogether comfortable. But he was getting better at it. 'Don't worry about Nick,' he said. 'He's quite happy, the way he is. And I will come to a party with you one day, I promise.'

She tilted her head back to look at him. 'When?'

'In the summer?'

He would be free in the summer. Nick would be back in Switzerland, he could see Sarah every day if that was what she wanted. They might even let him off Smeaton-on-Sea, they would be so chuffed to think he had acquired a regular girlfriend.

'I know!' She stepped back a pace, triumphantly punching him in the chest. 'The Midsummer Ball ... that's on a Friday! You can come to that!'

The Midsummer Ball had first been held some years

back to mark the joint centenaries of Astley College and the Lady Perceval School for Girls. Now it was an annual event, held one year at Astley, the next at Percy's. This year it was the turn of the girls' school to play host. The spectre began to haunt him. It wasn't only the fact that he couldn't dance – though he couldn't – it was the almost certain knowledge that the news would get back to Nick. Chris Seymour? With a *girl*? At a *DANCE*? Half the Astley sixth would be there. Probably half the fifth as well. There was bound to be some busybody who took it upon himself to let slip the information – 'Saw your mate at the dance the other night.' There were some people who would be only too happy to sow the seeds of dissension.

He knew that what he ought to do was find the courage to tell Nick himself. Really, it wouldn't be that difficult.

'My mother –' he could blame it on Louise – 'my mother has gone and promised I'll take this wretched girl to the midsummer thing.'

So if it weren't that difficult, why didn't he do it? Because he was a coward, that was why. He feared Nick's scorn, his reminder that he had 'told him so'; but more than that, he feared the future implications of such an admission. With the knowledge that Christopher had been out with Sarah once, how could Nick help but be watchful thereafter? Theirs was not a relationship which could encompass any third party. It was exclusive to themselves: intrusion could not be tolerated.

There were moments when he felt strong; almost strong enough to stand alone. These were the moments when he came closest to making his confession, but always, at the last minute, his nerve failed him. There were other moments – moments when some chance happening would remind him, all too forcibly, of his isolation within the school community – when his terrors returned to him in full measure, and at such moments as these he felt almost tempted to tell Sarah he had changed his mind. Almost, but not quite, for Sarah was his lifeline: without Nick he was lost, but without Sarah he had no hope.

And thus he vacillated, as he had vacillated so often before, and in the end achieved nothing. The evening before the dance Sarah rang him up.

'I just thought I'd run a final check,' she said. The Australian twang pitched pugnaciously into his ear. Sometimes he thought she affected an accent on purpose, just to sound more aggressive – Glenn didn't have one. (Though maybe, with monosyllables, it was more difficult to tell.) 'Is it still on?'

Now was his chance. 'Oh, Sal!' he could say. 'I'm glad you rang. I was going to call you . . . I'm afraid I'm not going to be able to make it tomorrow after all. Something's cropped up.'

And then she would say, 'What?' and he wouldn't be able to think of anything, and even if he did she wouldn't believe him, and then she would finally lose patience and find someone else. He was aware that he was hardly the ideal boyfriend.

'Of course it's still on,' he said. 'What do you take me for?'

She said, 'You really want to know?'

No; perhaps not. Whatever it was, he would prove her wrong.

'Don't forget,' he said, 'there's a little matter of a bet we made.' She had bet him 50p that when it came to it he wouldn't go. 'You'd better get busy on your money-box pig. You can hand over the loot when I come and pick you up.'

'When we get there,' she said. 'Not a minute before.'

He knew that even at this late stage she had her doubts. He was filled with a bright new determination, rock-solid and sure: tomorrow he would tell Nick that he was taking Sarah to the dance.

He woke on the morrow with his determination still intact; it was sabotaged by the absence of Nick from morning assembly. He continued absent throughout the morning. Old alarms came flooding back. Panic set in, as strong as ever.

At lunchtime he went out to the main road to telephone. (There was a public call box in the secretariat he could have used, but the secretaries were there and it put him off.) He dialled Nick's number and found himself speaking to the latest au pair. The Swede had departed and been replaced by a Spanish girl, who spoke about as much English as Christopher did Spanish, which wasn't very much at all. Tersely, he said: 'May I speak to Nick, please?'

'Nick?' she said. 'Am so sorry.'

They always said they were sorry; it didn't necessarily mean anything.

'I'd just like a quick word, that's all. Is he there?'

'He is here, but —'

'*Quiero conversar con él. Sí?*'

'*Sí*,' she said. She sounded dubious. 'Who speak, please?'

'Tell him it's Chris.'

'Chris. Hold, please. I will see.'

Within seconds, to his relief, he heard Nick's voice at the other end of the line: 'Hi.'

'What's happening? Why aren't you in school?'

'Didn't feel like it.'

'Why? What's wrong?'

'Just didn't feel like it. I can't explain over the phone. Come round tonight and I'll tell you.'

'Tonight? I can't manage tonight. I —' In his unprepared fluster, he plucked an excuse from the air. 'I promised my mother I'd stay in. She's got these people coming round. Ted and Mary. People she knew before she was married. I said I'd be there to meet them.'

'So come round after you've met them.'

'I can't do that, I've got to stay and have supper.'

'So come after supper.'

'I can't come after supper!' He spoke impatiently out of sheer fright. 'We won't be eating till about ten o'clock.'

There was a pause.

'Look, I could come round after school, just for half an hour.'

'Half an hour isn't any good. I'd sooner you didn't come at all.'

'Well, it's not my fault! Don't blame me! I don't want to spend the evening seeing people!'

'All right. It doesn't matter.'

'Why can't you tell me on the telephone?'

'I said it doesn't matter. Drop it. It's not important.'

'Well, I'll — I'll see you tomorrow. As usual. Yes?'

To this there was no reply: it took him a second or so to realize that that was because Nick had put the receiver down.

He spent a troubled afternoon veering between indignation that Nick should seem to imagine he could treat him like a lackey — *money can't buy everything in this life: that's a lesson we all have to learn* — and a growing conviction that he had either discovered his secret dalliance with Sarah or been told he had an incurable disease and would be dead by Christmas. The latter idea finally took a firm hold on him: Nick would be dead by Christmas and he, Christopher, would be friendless. Every day at school would be like this day at school. Every day –

'Hey!' Glenn had come lumbering up and banged him in the ribs. 'We got the use of the car. Come round your place, pick you up. Seven-thirty. OK?'

He nodded, preoccupied with thoughts of death and disease and life without Nick. As Glenn hunked off, he called after him: 'Tell Sal to bring her pig!'

Glenn stopped. 'What pig?'

'The one with the money in it . . . it's mine!' Silently he added: And I've earned every penny of it . . .

Before he left home, with Glenn and Sarah and the girl called Masha Kranz in Mel Sanderson's car, he did his best to disconnect the telephone by leaving the receiver off the hook and hiding it behind a pile of books. Louise and his grandmother were settled down to watch television: with any luck they would never notice.

The evening was not exactly what could be called an unqualified success. He was worried about Nick, worried at the possible consequences of telling him outright lies that could all too easily come to light, and all the time was conscious of people staring at him, whispering about him, wondering what he was doing there. Added to that, he didn't know how to dance. Sarah kept giggling and saying that the next time she would take him in hand before the event. Tony Forbes, who happened to overhear, winked and said, 'Who's a lucky boy?' but at the time he was in too high a state of anxiety to get the joke. Sarah obviously got it. She said, 'You don't have to go giving him ideas!'

'I should hope I don't,' said Forbes. 'I should hope he's already got them!'

He hadn't; he hadn't got any ideas of any kind whatsoever. His mind was a paralytic blank.

Randy Robson came up and leered and said, 'Where have I seen you before?' His partner sniggered appreciatively, as if he had just told a dirty joke. Christopher, at a loss as usual, contented himself with a feeble, 'Who knows?'

'Was that the randy one?' said Sarah. 'I didn't like the look of him.'

'Some girls reckon he's the cream.'

'Well, I suppose if they go for the big hairy types . . .' She grinned. 'I prefer intellectuals myself. Look, you see that girl over there? That's Angela Finch. The one I thought would do for Nickelarse. What d'you reckon?'

He looked, and shook his head. The girl was OK; there was nothing wrong with the girl.

'Just forget about Nick,' he said. He only wished he were capable of taking his own advice.

At the end of the evening Glenn suggested they drive into Bromley in search of some nightlife, but Masha Kranz said she couldn't, she'd promised her parents she'd go straight home. Christopher, nervous about the incapacitated telephone behind its flimsy barrier of books, said, 'Yeah, I guess I ought to be getting back as well.'

Glenn looked at him, sourly, through the driving mirror.

'Don't tell me you promised your grandmother?' said Sarah.

Hastily he said, 'No, it's my mother, she's got these people coming, I said I'd try to get back in time to meet them. But if you really –'

'Oh, forget it!' With noisy contempt, Glenn slammed the car into gear. 'Sal and I can go on our own.'

When he arrived back in Dalmally Road he found that his protective barrage of books had been removed and the receiver put back on the telephone. Apprehensively, he looked in on Louise to say goodnight. She asked him, briefly, about the dance, but was more concerned to tell him how his grandmother had come over 'very peculiar' and had had to go to bed.

'I'm really quite worried about her. I've been in two minds whether to call the doctor.'

She made no mention of having found the telephone off the hook, nor of anyone trying to ring him. In any case, he thought, there was no reason why Nick *should* ring him. They would be seeing each other tomorrow.

7

When he went down for breakfast next morning his grandmother was there, sitting in the kitchen sipping a cup of hot water. She was saying, 'Don't you worry about me, Lou. I'll be all right.'

'I still say you should have the doctor.' Louise turned, for support, to Christopher. 'What do you think? Don't you think your gran looks as if she should have the doctor?'

He studied her, briefly (his mind was still dwelling on the fiasco of last night. Had it really been worth it, jeopardizing his whole future with Nick just to please Sarah?) 'She looks OK to me,' he said. A bit parchmenty, perhaps, but otherwise much the same as usual.

'Well, I'm not happy,' said Louise. 'I don't like the thought of going out and leaving you.'

'You've got your work to do. That's more important than sitting here worrying about me.'

'I don't care, I think you should have someone with you. Christopher –' he stiffened, automatically – 'how about you?'

'Him?' His grandmother scoffed. 'He wouldn't be any use to anyone! Ask him to get you a cup of tea and he'd need instructions before he could make it. How did the dance go last night, anyway?'

'All right,' he said.

'Your friend rang while you were out. Did your mother tell you?'

He said, 'Friend?' The blood froze in his veins. 'Which friend?'

'Nick,' said Louise; as if he had any other. 'I'm sorry, I was worried about your gran. I forgot to tell you.'

'What —' his tongue flicked out over his lips — 'what did he want?'

'Wanted you,' said his grandmother. 'I told him, you weren't here. I said, he's taken Sarah to the school dance.'

The rage that welled within him was almost murderous. He wanted to lean across the table and pick her up by her horrible scrawny old neck and shake her till her brains started rattling and her false teeth fell out. He wanted to scream at her, 'You lousy interfering old bitch! You've just gone and screwed up the whole of my life!'

She sat back in her chair. A spasm crossed her face. He thought it was malicious glee at the havoc she had wrought, but Louise, hastening forward, said, 'Mum! Are you quite sure you won't let me call the doctor?'

'I've told you, Lou —' his grandmother's face was twisted with what he could now see was pain. She really was quite a curious sort of colour; more yellow than parchment. 'I'll be all right. It'll pass. Besides, I don't hold with doctors. Do you more harm than good, the most of them.'

'Well, if you're no better by tonight —'

'It'll be gone by tonight. Why is that boy standing

there like a lemon? Why doesn't he sit down and have his breakfast?'

He didn't feel like having breakfast. He didn't know what he felt like. The moment for murdering his grandmother had passed, and with the fury gone out of him he felt limp and shaky. He thought perhaps he was in a state of shock.

'Christopher –' Louise said it not so much hopefully as pleadingly – 'I suppose you couldn't possibly stay indoors this morning and go out later, when I get back?'

'No. I can't.' It was impossible. He had to get out there and face Nick; do his best to repair the damage. Already his brain was feverishly sifting through the possible excuses: a last-minute decision – no one else to take her – they insisted –

'I'd be back by four,' said Louise. 'That'd give you plenty of time to do whatever you want to do.'

'I'm going into Bromley. Four o'clock's too late. There wouldn't be any point in going then.' He snatched a piece of toast and rammed it into his mouth. 'I won't be long, I'll be back for lunch.'

'Don't hurry yourself on my account,' said his grandmother.

The bottom of Holt Hill was the point at which he and Nick traditionally met up; from there they could catch a bus which took them straight through to Bromley. Nick, who tended towards punctuality, was almost always the first to arrive: this morning there was no sign of him. Christopher stood waiting at the bus stop while the buses came and went. The minutes passed – five, ten, fifteen – and still there was no sign. He knew in his heart what he had known from the beginning: Nick was not going to come.

With the blood hammering in his ears, he set off up

the hill. Cowardice, when he reached Marden, almost turned him back: sheer desperation drove him on. It was the Spanish au pair who answered the door. He stood on the front step conducting an urgent conversation in pidgin Spanish, the upshot of which seemed to be that Nick was out. Everybody was out: the house was empty.

He left a message for Nick to ring him, and glumly trailed off again, down the hill. The day stretched meaninglessly, endlessly, before him. He had no inclination to go into Bromley without Nick. He would feel awkward, going into their normal haunts on his own. People would look at him, wondering where Nick was. It occurred to him that maybe, just maybe, he might have gone into Weedon's as usual, without bothering to wait for Christopher. Nick was self-sufficient: it wouldn't worry him that people might be whispering about him, speculating where the other half of the partnership was. Perhaps he ought to go in, just to have a quick look. If Nick wasn't there he could always come out again.

A grey drizzle had begun to fall. He hunched himself into his anorak and took up his previous position at the bus stop. While he was standing there, Tony Forbes and John Newman passed him, on bicycles. Newman flapped a hand and called out, 'All on yer own, luv?' in a pseudo north country accent. Forbes, who seemed a bit embarrassed, just grinned and nodded.

Nick wasn't in Weedon's. He thought for a moment that he might already have been and gone, until Stuart Fordyce, catching sight of him as he made his way back out, raised an eyebrow and said, 'So what's happened to the other one this morning?' which told him that Nick hadn't been in at all.

He went the rounds of the bookshops, without any

success; likewise the library, both reference section and lending. It was still only half-past eleven. He didn't feel like going home, but he couldn't think of anything else to do. He supposed he could go somewhere and have a coffee. That would kill a bit of time.

He walked past three possible places before he was able to nerve himself to go into one, and then it was a seedy sandwich bar the size of a broom cupboard where they didn't even have chairs or tables but only plastic trays stuck on the tops of poles. He bought a polystyrene cup of what passed for coffee (it looked more like untreated sewage) and stood self-conscious by a plastic tray. It was one of those days when everyone was staring. He had noticed the phenomenon before. You walked fifty yards along the High Street and as many people stopped to look at you, some of them quite insolently, until you knew for certain that your flies were undone and everything on view, and you had to keep groping at yourself or taking surreptitious peeks in shop windows. He had once mentioned it to Sarah, during one of their Rik Harper evenings, when he occasionally felt bold enough to make such sort of confessions. (He could never have confessed it to Nick.) Sarah had surprised him by admitting that it had happened to her, too.

'Only it's not my flies being undone, it's thinking that I might suddenly have come on and be *goring* over everything.'

He had been amazed that he was not the only one to suffer from embarrassing obsessions. Comforted, too; and intrigued.

'But that couldn't really happen,' he said, 'could it?'
'What d'you mean, *could* it? It does!'
'What, and you don't know about it?'

'Well, you would know, pretty soon, but you mightn't realize till it was too late . . . I can tell you, it's far worse for us than it is for you!'

It had never struck him before. He had never until then paused to consider what it might be like, to be a girl. Of course he knew in theory, from books and biology lessons; but Sarah had opened his eyes to some of the reality.

Thinking of Sarah made him think of Nick, made him desperate all over again. He left his coffee unfinished and went back out to find a telephone box. This time there was no reply, even from the au pair.

Back in Holt Wood, for want of anything better to do, he called in at the Merrie Kettle hoping for a free lunch. Sometimes if they weren't too busy they would let him sit at the staff table in the annexe and clear up whatever wasn't going too well on the menu. Today they were only medium busy, but Louise came bustling red-faced and bloody-aproned out of the kitchen to tell him to go home.

'I asked you, Christopher . . . I already asked you! Your gran needs someone there. You promised me, you said you'd be home by lunchtime, I've been relying on you, I've –'

'Yeah, yeah!' he said. 'OK, OK!' She didn't have to make a big thing of it. 'I forgot, I'm sorry.'

'How can you forget, when your grandmother –'

'What's the matter with her, anyway?'

'I don't know, but I'm very worried about her. She keeps being sick and she's in a lot of pain. If she's any worse when you get back, you must give me a ring. Immediately. You must promise me!'

'OK,' he said.

His grandmother was sitting in her accustomed place

in front of the television. She looked to him the same as she had looked this morning, but he said, 'You all right?' just to satisfy his conscience.

'I'm all right,' she said. 'Thank you.' He got the impression she didn't like him asking any more than he liked having to ask. Nevertheless, he wasn't completely lacking in a sense of duty.

'Can I get you anything?'

'Such as what?'

'Cup of tea? Bowl of soup? Boiled egg?'

'That's right,' she said. 'Give me salla monella.'

Ungracious as ever. He resisted the temptation to point out, as he had pointed out a dozen times before, that it was salmonella.

'So which do you want?' he said.

'I'll have a cup of tea – if you think you can manage it.'

As he took her her tea, very casually he said: 'Any phone calls while I was out?'

'If you mean, has he rung, the answer is no, he hasn't. Had his nose put out of joint, I daresay. And a good thing, too.'

He had another dangerous moment of wanting to pick her up and shake her.

At three-thirty the telephone rang. He rushed to get it (his grandmother made no move) but it was only Sarah wanting to talk about last night.

'That guy was a real creep, wasn't he? That Randy one. Glenn seems to think he's OK, but Glenn is just totally un-re-liable where men are concerned ... all the nice ones he calls poufs, all the really ghastly ones, all the Rambo types that I wouldn't touch with a barge pole, he says are OK.'

Her prattle, which normally he enjoyed because it spared him the effort of having to make conversation, today only annoyed him. He wanted her to get off the line in case Nick should be trying to ring. He didn't mean to make it obvious, but it must have come across without him being aware of it for after a bit she said, 'Well, since you seem so interested I won't bore you any longer. You coming round tomorrow?'

Was he? Or wasn't he? If Nick would only ring – if he could just get in touch with him –

'Look, you don't have to,' said Sarah. 'It's not a royal command or anything.'

He mumbled that he would if he could but he wasn't quite sure.

'Suit yourself,' she said. She sounded just like his grandmother.

He went into the sitting-room to check how she was. She hadn't drunk her tea, she said it was 'too milky', it turned her stomach.

'Who was that on the telephone? Sarah? Didn't sound to me the way a young man should talk to his girlfriend. Very high and mighty. No way to treat a young woman.'

He picked up her teacup and took it away to the kitchen. He didn't offer her anything else. He reckoned if she could listen in on other people's telephone conversations there couldn't be too much wrong with her.

He rang Nick's number three more times during the course of the next half-hour without getting any reply. At four o'clock Louise arrived back and was told about the cup of tea: 'I said he wouldn't know how to make it. Turned my stomach. I couldn't drink it.'

'I drank it OK,' said Christopher.

Louise made shushing motions at him. Afterwards, in the kitchen, she said, 'Try not to get cross with her.

I know she's being difficult, but she's not at all well. If she's no better by Monday I'm having the doctor in.'

At seven o'clock, as usual on a Saturday, he went round to Marden. If Nick were there, he would be expecting him; and if he weren't there – well, if he weren't there at least he might be able to find out where he was.

He was relieved when the door was opened by Susan Sheringham. He was always slightly at a loss with Nick's mother – she seemed, for some reason, to find him a source of amusement – but at least she spoke English.

'Hello!' she said. She stood, looking down at him from the top step. She had a glass in her hand and there were vivid splashes of colour across her cheeks. It struck him that she was swaying slightly, or maybe it was only an optical illusion. 'Where's Nick?' she said. 'Isn't he with you?'

'No.' Desperation, for once, unlocked his tongue. 'I haven't seen him all day. I thought he was round here.'

'He's not round here. I thought he was with you.' Her speech, quite definitely, was slurred. 'He went off early this morning before any of us were up. I thought perhaps you'd gone into town or something.'

'No,' he said. 'I haven't seen him.'

'Isn't that odd? I wonder where he can have gone?'

He wasn't sure whether she expected him to supply an answer or not.

'He didn't go into Weedon's,' he said.

'Weedon's?' She repeated it, vaguely.

'The record shop we go in.'

'Oh, yes . . . Weedon's. Perhaps he's gone up to town. What do you think?'

'I don't know,' said Christopher. 'I haven't seen him since Thursday.'

'Ah ... so you won't have heard the news?' She leaned towards him, breathing brandy fumes. He thought it was brandy; it might have been whisky. Anyway, spirits of some kind. 'Swiss Granny died. It was quite sudden. We all had a terrible shock. Nick more than anyone. He didn't say much, but then he never does, does he? Do you find that? He never shows what he's feeling. Never lets on.'

He mumbled his agreement: Nick never did let on.

'I do so hope he hasn't done anything foolish. He loved Swiss Granny. They were really close.'

He mumbled again; embarrassed, not knowing what to say.

'She was *my* mother, you know.'

He hadn't known. Nick had never talked much about Swiss Granny.

'Nick was her favourite – her favourite of all the grandchildren. She and Nick – thick as thieves. Went everywhere together. Talked together. Hours on end. At home – stumm! Can't get a word out of him. You get a word out of him?'

He hesitated, not sure Nick would like him standing here talking about him with his mother.

'Anyway. Friday morning, phone rang. Switzerland. Your mother. Passed away. In her sleep.' She frowned. 'Did Nick go to school that day?'

'No,' said Christopher.

'No. That's right; he stayed at home. Played the piano. All day. He won't tell, you see. Won't talk to you. Me, I'm quite the opposite. I give out.' She flung an arm wide. For a dreadful moment he thought she was going to fall down the steps on top of him. 'Nick holds it all in. He's like his father; they simmer. Do you know what I mean?'

He said, 'Yeah. I know what you mean.'

'Won't ever let go. So silly. He must be like a coiled spring . . . just like a coiled spring.'

He said, 'When he gets back, would you ask him to call me?'

'I will. I'll leave a message for him. I'm going out myself, but I'll stick a big note on his door, where he can't miss it.'

She smiled, brilliantly. He suddenly perceived that she was what people called an attractive woman. Nick, with his dark hair and rather set, narrow face, took after his father, physically as well as emotionally. Susan Sheringham was a redhead, thin as a rake with huge burning violet eyes set within deep hollows in a face curiously triangular in shape. He had always accepted, without thinking too much about it, that mothers must inevitably look like Louise: faded and grey and middle-aged. He supposed there must have been a time when Louise hadn't looked faded and grey, but he couldn't actually remember it.

He walked slowly back to Dalmally Road, thinking about Nick and Swiss Granny. *I hope he hasn't done anything foolish* . . . but Nick wouldn't. He was too much in control of things. He wondered if he had cried when he had heard that Swiss Granny had died. He dismissed the idea: it simply wasn't possible to imagine Nick breaking down.

He spent the evening sitting in front of the television mindlessly watching quiz shows and other assorted junk, waiting for the telephone to ring. The only thing which made the evening bearable was that his grandmother had gone to bed. Louise said again, 'I'm really very worried about her.' He grunted: it was all the sympathy he could muster. He had worries enough of his own.

At eleven o'clock, when Nick still hadn't rung, he telephoned Marden: there was no reply. Louise said yet again, as she turned off the television for the night, 'If your grandmother isn't any better by Monday I'm going to call the doctor whether she likes it or not.'

On Sunday morning, on his way round to Hawthorn Avenue, he made a detour and called again at Marden. He thought, at first, that the house was empty; either that or that no one was going to answer. When at last the door opened it was Nick's father who stood there. He was wearing a dressing-gown and pyjamas, with his hair all ruffled and sleep furrows engraven on one cheek. He didn't look too pleased to see Christopher on his doorstep. Possibly he didn't know who he was. He said, 'What sort of time do you call this?'

'Sorry,' said Christopher. It was nine o'clock. 'I just wondered if Nick had come back.'

'Come back from where?'

He said lamely, 'Yesterday.'

'I didn't know he'd gone anywhere yesterday. He's probably down the road in the God house, lighting candles and confessing his sins.'

Nick's father made as if to close the door. Desperately, standing his ground, Christopher said: 'It's just that he was going to ring me.'

'Was he? Well, I expect he will when he gets back. Now, if you'll excuse me –'

This time, the door was very firmly shut. Walking back down the road, to catch the bus for Hawthorn Avenue, he passed the Catholic church which Nick attended. (Mr Sheringham obviously wasn't into religion: it must have come from Swiss Granny's side of the family.) He paused for a moment, but didn't like to go in. They were probably in the middle of a service, and besides it might seem like spying. In any case, he had to be round at Sarah's by half-ten. He had made a vague promise, the night of the dance, that he would go up to town with her, to the Museum of London, for a project she had to do. He had never been to the Museum of London. At least it would be a new experience.

The Museum would have been fine, were it not for the crowds and the fact that he couldn't stop thinking about Nick. (*Had* he come back? *Was* he in church? *Why* hadn't he rung?) Sarah didn't terribly seem to mind the crowds, or perhaps she was just more skilled than he at burrowing her way to the front. When he grumbled, she accused him of being a misery and anti-social. They argued about it all the way back to Waterloo.

'What d'you expect? Expect them to close the place to everyone except you?'

'All I said was I don't like crowds!'

'Don't like *people*!'

'I do like people!'

'You don't like people.'

'I don't like them *en masse*.'

'Don't like them at *all*!'

On the train to Holt Wood they developed the argument one stage further until it became a vicious row. Sarah said he was not only a misery and anti-social but boring and self-absorbed. She accused him of behaving like a capitalist lackey, 'Running about after Nick . . . smarming over him, *creeping* up to him . . . *oh* –' She mimicked him, in the middle of a (fortunately empty) compartment – '*Whatever you want, Nick, whatever you say, Nick, kiss your shoes and lick your arse, Nick!* It's a wonder your knees don't get sore, all the crawling you do . . . you ought to buy special *crawling* pads!'

He flushed, angrily. 'It just so happens,' he said, 'that Nick's grandmother died last week. He wanted me to go round there Friday night but I didn't because I'd already arranged to go out with you.'

'Oh, big deal!' she said, heavily sarcastic.

'Yeah, it was a big deal! He was feeling dead rough. If you're not allowed to show ordinary human concern for someone you've –' He was going to have said, 'For someone you've known a lot longer than I've known you,' but she cut in ahead of him.

'I should've thought it'd be more to the point if you showed a bit of ordinary human concern for your own grandmother! Your mum rang up last night in a terrible state, saying about how ill she was and how she wouldn't have the doctor.'

'So she won't have the doctor! So that's her problem! What am I supposed to do about it?'

'You could at least *care!*'

'I do care.'

'You call that caring?'

'Call what caring?'

'Just going out and doing your own thing – not even being there. God!' cried Sarah. 'You're so unfeeling!'

He wasn't unfeeling; not in a general way. But he didn't see why he should be expected to weep tears over someone who had spent the whole of his life telling him he was unnatural. He said as much to Sarah but she only snapped pettishly at him that 'You are unnatural! You're the most unnatural person I've ever met! Care more about your boyfriend than about your own grandmother!'

By the time they left the train they were no longer on speaking terms. Sarah, tight-lipped, set off in the direction of Hawthorn Avenue; Christopher headed for Dalmally Road. He was supposed to have been going back with her for a meal. He wondered how she would explain his absence and what Helen Sanderson would say. It would all get back to his grandmother, of course.

He scuffled, broodingly, along the High Street. 'So you've fallen out with Sarah, then.' He could hear her already; the triumph ('I always knew he wouldn't be able to keep a girlfriend') doing battle with the desire to apportion blame and condemn.

'All your fault, I dare say. I'm only surprised she put up with you as long as she did.'

After the things that Sarah had accused him of he hardly liked to call round yet again at Marden; besides, he was scared of Nick's father answering the door again. He decided to wait till he got home and see if Nick had rung.

His grandmother and Louise were sitting in front of the television. His grandmother was looking decidedly yellow. He hung about for a bit, hoping that one of them would volunteer some information without his being forced to ask, and then, when neither of them did, said carelessly, 'I was expecting a call from someone at school. I suppose they didn't ring yet?'

'Nobody rang,' said Louise.

'Oh. Well – in that case I'd better go and give them a bell.' Carefully he closed the sitting-room door behind him, even though in the summer months his grandmother liked it left open so she could hear what was going on. (In the winter months she complained bitterly if he only just left it slightly ajar – 'What's the matter with that boy? Born in a field?')

It was Nick's brother who answered the telephone. He would almost rather it had been anybody but him; even the au pair. He had known for a long time that Gerald held him in contempt.

He said, 'Could I speak to Nick, please?'

'I don't know if he's in. Hang on, I'll go and see. Who is it?'

'Could you tell him it's Chris.'

Within seconds, Gerald was back. 'Sorry.' His voice came clipped and curt down the line. 'He doesn't want to talk to anyone.'

The receiver was put down before he had a chance to protest.

Monday morning he was woken at the appalling hour of six o'clock by Louise coming into his room. She said, 'Your grandmother's been up all night. I'm going to call the doctor.'

He said, 'Good idea,' and waited for her to go away again. Instead, she sat herself on the edge of the bed and started tracing patterns with her finger on the duvet.

'Your gran doesn't want me to. She says it's just something she's eaten.'

'All that junk food.'

'But it's been going on for days! And it's just getting worse. I can't go off to work and leave her in this state.'

'Well,' he said, 'call him, then.' That's what doctors were for, wasn't it?

'I know why she doesn't want me to.' Louise's right index finger swirled in nervous circles. 'She's scared. In case they – discover something. In case they

131

want to operate. You can understand it, at her age.'

He said, 'Right.'

'But she can't go on like this! It's ridiculous!'

There was a silence.

'I shall ring him as soon as surgery opens.'

He grunted.

'I've half a mind to do it right away, only I hate to call them out of hours. It seems so unfair, when they work so hard.'

'And get paid so much.'

'They ought to get paid so much, the job they do! People ringing them in the middle of the night. They deserve every penny of it. I'm going to make a cup of tea; do you want one?'

At nine o'clock, Louise rang the surgery.

'They've promised he'll come round as soon as he can, but he can't tell whether it's going to be this morning or this afternoon. I think I'd better ring and say I can't get into work today. I think that's best.'

He offered – since the Monday after the Midsummer Ball was Open Day, which he never bothered to attend – to stay in himself, but Louise seemed to think it wasn't a good idea.

'She could be sick again; you wouldn't know what to do.'

'I'm not useless!' he said.

'No, of course you're not, I didn't mean that, but she'd be happier if I were here. You go out and do whatever you want to do.'

There wasn't any point in going out; he had nowhere to go to, no one to go with. He said, 'I'll stay in and keep you company.' Louise grew pink. She pressed his arm and said, 'That's nice of you.' He then felt guilty, so that instead of going up to his room and shutting the door he felt impelled to martyr himself by staying downstairs and talking to her.

It was lunchtime when the doctor came. He was upstairs for about ten minutes, and murmuring in the hall with Louise for a further five.

'Christopher –' Louise appeared, looking flustered. 'Pop down the road and get these prescriptions for your gran, there's a good boy.'

'What happened?' he said. 'All that junk food?'

'The doctor thinks it's an obstruction.'

'What sort of obstruction?'

Louise pinched her lips together. 'A growth.'

'Oh. You mean –'

'Sh!' She put up a hand, agitated. 'Your gran doesn't know. She thinks it's an ulcer. The doctor's going to call tomorrow with an appointment for the hospital. He seems to think they'll take her in pretty quickly. I must get back to her, she'll think we've been talking about her.'

He tried, as he walked to the nearest chemist in the High Street, to review his feelings about his grandmother in the light of what he had just heard, but all he could think of was going back to school tomorrow: whether Nick would be there, whether he would be sufficiently recovered from the shock of losing Swiss Granny to resume normal relations. He held on to the one ray of hope that he had. Gerald hadn't said 'He doesn't want to talk to *you*' but 'He doesn't want to talk to *any*one.'

He arrived back with the prescriptions to find his grandmother in the sitting-room, wrapped in a blanket and bright yellow.

'Where are my tablets?' she said.

He handed them to her. He tried to make himself

say, 'How are you feeling?' but the words wouldn't come.

'By the way,' said Louise, 'Sarah called round. She left this for you.'

She handed him an envelope. On the outside was a sticker saying STOP ANIMAL EXPERIMENTS. He opened it, curious. Inside, on a single sheet of paper, she had typed the first eight lines of a poem:

Since there's no help, come let us kiss and part,
Nay, I have done: you get no more of me
And I am glad, yea glad with all my heart,
That thus so cleanly I my self can free.
Shake hands for ever, cancel all our vows,
And when we meet at any time again,
Be it not seen in either of our brows,
That we one jot of former love retain.

At the bottom, in handwriting, was the instruction, heavily underlined: **PTO**. He did so: his cheeks turned scarlet. Still in handwriting, Sarah had scrawled,

' "Your true love hath your heart" – and it seems there's nothing I can do about it.'

'Love letter?' said his grandmother.

Idiotically, without thinking, anxious only that no one should see it, he crumpled the page into a ball.

'Lovers' tiff,' said his grandmother. She nodded, sagely. 'Had to happen, sooner or later. I'm only surprised it lasted as long as it did. Bright girl like that, get anyone she wanted.'

He opened his mouth, remembered just in time that she might have a growth, and left the room before he lost control of himself.

Upstairs, he lay face downward on his bed, thinking

about Sarah. She was his lifeline. Without Sarah there was no hope – but without Nick he was lost. Nick was his friend; his only friend. Life without Nick just wouldn't be bearable. If he had to sacrifice one or the other, there was no doubt in his mind which one it would be. For all that –

Your true love hath your heart . . .

But it wasn't like that! It wasn't *like* that!

He thumped at the pillow as downstairs the telephone started to ring. He was out on the landing in a split milli-second, but Louise was already there. She turned, and held out the receiver.

'It's for you.'

Joyously, two at a time, he rocketed down the stairs. 'Nick?'

It wasn't Nick, it was the library.

8

He was late arriving at school on Tuesday. He slipped into the assembly hall in time to catch the end of old Bogey's usual post-Open Day rapture – 'Our royal patron, the Duchess of Gloucester . . .'

Anxiously he scanned the ranks of sixth formers, regally seated on chairs down two sides of the hall. His heart bounded in relief: Nick was there, halfway down the row, next to John Newman.

Old Bogey's voice droned to a close. They would conclude, he said, by offering up a prayer of thanksgiving.

'Almighty God, we offer our thanks for another successful year. We ask you to keep safe our gracious patron, HRH the Duchess of Gloucester –'

There were some things Christopher might have prayed for, but the safety of the Duchess of Gloucester was not one of them. He concentrated his energies, instead, on beaming mental messages to Nick, who surely must have noticed his absence and be wondering where he had got to.

The messages either failed to reach their target or the target chose to ignore them. Nick continued to sit with

dipped head, the same as everyone else, seemingly pray-
ing for HRH. He never knew how much Nick actually
believed in all this religious stuff, in spite of being a
Catholic; but even if he believed wholeheartedly he
certainly could have no more interest than Christopher
in the welfare of an unknown duchess.

Christopher redoubled his efforts. The pray-in came
to an end, members of the staff stood up and filed from
the hall, followed by the sixth. He succeeded, at last, in
catching Nick's eye. To his cold horror, Nick looked
straight through him and out the other side, for all the
world as if he had ceased to exist.

In a state of shock, he fell in behind John Newman
and trailed in his wake to the common room to col-
lect his books for the period of double English which
started the day. Nick was there before him, standing
at his locker. As Christopher approached he slammed
the door shut and strode past, ostentatiously avoiding
all contact. Christopher didn't dare to say anything, in
a room full of people.

He snatched up his books and elbowed his way
back out. Nick, already, was at the top of the stairs.
He called after him – 'Hey, Nick!' The silence was
deafening.

A bunch of second years came twittering down
on him. He plunged through them, scattering them
unceremoniously. One of them, in cheeky parody of
old Bogey, shrieked, 'We will not have *running* on the
stairs!' and they all snickered. By the time he reached
the top, Nick had disappeared.

The English studio at the end of the corridor was
empty. Christopher sank down into one of the double
desks inside the door; in twos and threes the rest of the
class came shambling in, followed by the senior English

master, known inevitably, his name being Marriner, as the Ancient M. Nick arrived late. He muttered something, Christopher couldn't hear what, by way of apology, looked round the room, noted where Christopher was sitting and coolly and deliberately trod a path to the far side.

Christopher's gaze followed him, hot with shame and resentment. Why was Nick doing this to him? Exposing him to public ridicule. Already he could see people exchanging glances, speculating: wondering. People expected them to sit together. They always sat together; they always had done. If Nick had any grievance he should keep it private and between the two of them, not lay it bare for the rest of the world to gloat over.

Trembling, he bent his head over his books. He had his grandmother to thank for this.

Nick successfully avoided him for the rest of the morning. Not until lunchtime did Christopher finally manage to force a confrontation.

'Nick!' He ran after him along the Broad Walk, catching at his sleeve to slow him down. Nick jerked his arm away, angrily.

'Do you mind not pawing at me?'

'Sorry.'. He shouldn't have done that; he knew Nick had an aversion to being touched. 'I just wanted to s–'

'I'd prefer that you didn't, if it's all the same to you.'

'But it's about your grandmother!' He did a little hop to keep up. 'I'm really s–'

'I said I would prefer that you didn't. What's the matter? Don't you understand plain English?'

He swallowed. 'I just wish you'd told me. On Friday . . . I wish you'd said.'

'Why? What difference would it have made?'

'All the difference in the world! I'd have come round, you know I would!'

'Do I?' said Nick.

'Well, of course I would!' There was a silence. 'Look, I can explain about Friday. It's not like you think. Honestly! We did have people coming, it's just that at the last minute s–'

'I don't wish to know.'

'But you've got to know! You've got to listen to me!'

'I haven't *got*,' said Nick, 'to do anything.'

'You could at least give me the benefit of the doubt! All I'm trying –'

'All you're trying to do is salvage something which has been wrecked beyond any hope of repair. Why do you have to keep on lying? *Now?* When it doesn't matter any more? Is it such a habit with you that you can't stop?'

'Lying?' said Christopher. He chewed in frenzy at his right index finger, tearing off a large flap of skin. 'What do you mean, lying?'

'You know perfectly well what I mean.'

'I don't! I'm trying to explain, only –'

'*Listen!* You!' Nick came to a full stop. There, in the middle of the Broad Walk, he turned at last to face Christopher. 'Let me just put you out of your grovelling, snivelling misery . . . I *know* you'd arranged weeks ago to take the girl to the dance because your grandmother took great pleasure in telling me so . . . she practically gave me your joint life histories for the past few months. So just spare yourself the contortions, OK?'

Fear invaded him, shooting tentacles through his veins. He tore another flap of skin from his finger and blood spurted out over his nail. He hadn't known his grandmother had gone that far. He could imagine her revelling, happy that she might be causing trouble between them.

'The thing is –' he sprang forward, keeping pace with Nick – 'if you'd just explained! If you'd told me on the telephone! I'd have let her go to the damn thing by herself! I didn't want to take her, I was pushed into it. It's only because she's a sort of relation – because she hasn't been here long, she doesn't know anyone –'

Nick looked at him, scornfully.

'If it's any help,' said Christopher, 'I shan't be seeing her again. I've finished with her. It's all come to an end! It's reached a natural conclusion.'

'Not the only thing to have done so,' said Nick.

He ignored the implications of that. They were more than he could take.

'What is it you're mad at me for? For not telling you? Or for going out with her in the first place? I would have told you, if it had been serious – but it wasn't! It wasn't ever anything!' It hadn't been anything; not when compared with the world he inhabited with Nick. He tried, haltingly, to say so: Nick cut him short.

'Let's get one thing straight: I am not *mad* at you. I don't care enough to be *mad* at you. As far as I'm concerned you can go out with anyone you choose. It's quite immaterial to me. I am not your keeper. You're perfectly free to do what you like and go where you like. I no longer care what you do. From now on I just want to be left alone.'

'Nick, for God's sake!'

Nick stopped again; so abruptly that Christopher almost cannoned into him. He checked himself just in time.

'Did you hear what I said?'

140

'But – but Guy and – and Oliver –'

'Guy and Oliver,' said Nick. His lip curled. 'Who are they? Friends of yours?'

The following week was, quite simply, the worst of his entire life so far. Nick, as he had long suspected, appeared to be self-sufficient. He was teaching himself Spanish and spent much of his time in the Upper School library. Any feeble attempts at negotiation were coolly repelled: he seemed not to care, or maybe not to notice, that the rest of the sixth were eagerly keeping the situation under review.

It was Christopher's nightmare turned to reality. His isolation was now complete. Rejected by Nick, shunned by his fellows, he couldn't help wondering . . . had it always been like this?

It seemed to him, looking back, that it hadn't. Faint, disturbing memories came to him, from his first term at Astley, of swinging upside down from the hot water pipes in the junior cloakroom with Harry Morgan, of all people. Had he ever really been close to Harry Morgan? It was such a long time ago. The years from eleven to sixteen – almost seventeen, now – they stretched behind him, back into the dim distance of his childhood, of his infancy, of days long vanished from his mind.

'I remember when he was a babby,' his grandmother used, embarrassingly, to say. 'Lovely, he was then. Little curly top, we used to call you.'

Small wonder *that* had vanished. But what of all those other days? The other days they told him about, when he had climbed on old Annie Smith's coal bunker and chased round the back alleys and played at marbles with the boys up the road?

The boys up the road – some of them – still lived up the road, but they had all transferred to the comprehensive and scarcely even acknowledged him, these days, as they went about their business. For all the communication there was between them you would never have guessed they had had the common experience of being sworn at by Annie Smith and ganged up against by the boys from Ridgemount. Christopher had once said 'Hi' to Pete Matthews as they crossed paths on the way home from school, and Pete Matthews had looked at him as if he were a stranger, plainly at a loss. Why should this weirdo open his mouth at him?

For years, now, Christopher hadn't spoken; not because he felt superior (which was what his grandmother claimed – 'Thinks himself too good for the likes of ordinary folk') but because he was scared of being snubbed. He guessed Harry Morgan would snub him if he were to try muscling in on his lot. He had left it too late. Once a freak, always a freak. Whatever had gone wrong could not easily be repaired.

He stuck it out for almost a fortnight. His grandmother had gone into hospital and was waiting to have tests, only they kept postponing it, putting it off from one day to the next – probably, Christopher suspected, because she was old and disposable and was going to die soon anyway; but for whatever reason it upset Louise, who worried that she ought to complain to someone but was scared to do so for fear of antagonizing those in authority. She kept wringing her hands and saying, 'This is where one needs a man.'

He said, 'Do you want me to go and do it for you?', but at first she didn't take the suggestion seriously and then when he repeated it she just said, 'No, not you! It needs a grown-up.'

He had made the offer; let nobody say he didn't try.

One Friday lunchtime, walking into the common room, he caught the tail end of a conversation between Glenn Sanderson and Pete Dossett, one of Harry Morgan's mob. From Pete Dossett he heard the words 'finally split', and from Glenn, in response, 'Coupla poufs!' They buttoned up the minute he appeared. He knew they had been talking about him and Nick.

That afternoon, in the last period of the day, which was German, he resorted to the tactics of a first former. He scribbled a fierce note on a sheet of A4 – *This is ridiculous! We can't carry on like this. At least give me some sign that you're prepared to meet me half-way* – folded it, dropped his books on the floor, and under cover of retrieving them managed to deposit the note on Nick's desk without, he thought, anyone being any the wiser. He watched, tense and nervous, as Nick opened it out. There was a pause; then slowly, with an air of terrible ennui, Nick closed a hand over the paper, crushed it, and dropped it behind him on to the floor.

Sick and shaking, Christopher clawed it up. People nearby were looking at him, craning, wondering what was going on. He knew he wouldn't be able to take much more of it.

Over the weekend he went with Louise to visit his grandmother. He hadn't wanted to, but there was no way he could decently get out of it. He had expected her to be her usual rebarbative self, slagging off everyone within earshot, convinced they were trying to poison her; instead, he was somewhat shaken to discover that she had overnight become unbearably humble, almost abasing herself in her efforts to please.

'I don't want to cause any bother,' she kept saying.

The new persona didn't suit her. It stripped her of all those characteristics, repulsive though they were, which had made her recognizably herself, diminishing her to a shrivelled shred of what she had been: anxious to propitiate, devoid of dignity.

Louise asked about the tests she was supposed to be having.

'They'll do them,' said his grandmother, 'in their own good time. I dare say there's a waiting list; we all have to take our turn. There's people more important than me around.'

When Louise, given courage perhaps by Christopher's presence, suggested speaking to one of the nurses, his grandmother became agitated and started plucking at the bedclothes with skeletal fingers, saying she didn't want to cause bother, she didn't want any fuss made, they would do what they felt to be right.

'Just leave them, Lou. They know what they're about. They're the experts, not us.'

He had never thought to find his grandmother pathetic; he felt that he would rather not have known.

On Monday, Nick was not at school. The remainder of the week was rendered hideous beyond belief by his continued absence. At least when he was there, there was some faint, lingering chance that he might relent and agree to a reconciliation. People kept coming up and slyly asking, 'What's happened to your mate, then?' Knowing full well that he and Nick hadn't been speaking for the last fortnight.

On Thursday he was summoned to the Presence and interrogated for half an hour by Bogey on the subject of Nick and Nick's state of mind, as if Nick would ever deign to expose his state of mind to Christopher.

'I understand –' the Headmaster leaned back in his

chair with his hands placed carefully and artistically upon the padded arms – 'he has recently been upset by the death of his grandmother?'

Christopher made a mumbling sound.

'Has he spoken to you at all about this? Have you ever discussed it?'

'We don't really talk about things like that … personal things.'

'Mm.' The Headmaster swivelled thoughtfully for a while. 'It has not escaped my notice – or, let us say, it has been brought to my attention – that the two of you have not been seen together nearly so much as hitherto. Is there any particular reason for this?'

Christopher drew himself up and looked the Headmaster straight in the eye through the lower half of his bifocals. 'You told us not to. We're only doing what you said.'

Old Bogey made irritable noises with his tongue. 'Come, come, Seymour! I didn't mean you to quarrel like a couple of first form children. I was pleased, by the way, to hear that you were present at the Midsummer Ball. I had hoped for a sight of you on Open Day; but at least we are making progress. Of a sort.'

On the Friday he tried to stay in bed. He told Louise he was running a temperature, but she didn't believe him. She felt his forehead, in perfunctory fashion, and said, 'Don't be silly, Christopher! There's nothing wrong with you. Get up and go to school. You can't miss classes just because you're feeling a bit under the weather.'

He said, 'There aren't any classes to miss. It's all over bar the shouting, we break up next week.'

'I don't care. You get up, I'm not going to stand here arguing with you. I have other things to worry about. Your grandmother's having her tests today. That's far more important than you grizzling about your temperature.'

In English, the Ancient Marriner beamed approvingly.

'I hear you are all off next weekend to visit Kipling's abode . . . well, now! I am a great admirer of Kipling. He has fallen somewhat out of favour during these latter years, but I can personally recommend him if you are after a good yarn . . . never disparage the good yarn! If anyone cares to follow up the visit with some holiday reading, I shall be greatly interested to hear what you make of him.'

Christopher hadn't even known there was going to be a visit. No one had approached him. They had long accepted that it was a waste of effort asking either him or Nick.

As he sat in the common room later, having his ears blasted by Screaming Virago (Sal hadn't cared for Screaming Virago: she had said they were 'Glenn's sort of music, not mine') he overheard a conversation taking place behind him. He overheard a lot of conversations these days, now that he was on his own; since nobody spoke to him, it was the only way he could ever glean any information. The conversation was between Forbes and Newman. They were making arrangements to meet up at a disco that evening. Forbes was going with the girl called Debbie Mander: Newman was taking Sal. He had been out with her last weekend, he said. He reckoned it would only be a question of time before she let him go the whole way. 'Hot knickers,' he said. Forbes said he wasn't surprised. He intimated that the last few weeks must have been 'a bit of a let down' for her.

'To say the least,' said Newman.

'To *say* the least,' said Forbes.

At that point, one of them must have turned round and seen who was sitting behind them because they both shut up.

That afternoon he wondered what it would be like to commit suicide. It was something he had often wondered about, in an idle, academic fashion. That afternoon he pondered the actual practicalities of it. He knew he was too much afraid of physical pain to hang himself or cut an artery; there had to be an easier way than that. In the old days, in books, it had been gas ovens. Gas ovens or the railway line. Gas ovens were out, the stuff wasn't toxic any more, and he knew he would never have the guts to chuck himself in front of a train. There were always aspirins, of course.

The idea began to take hold of him. He wondered how many bottles he would need; whether one would be sufficient or whether it would simply paralyse him or turn him into a vegetable. Better buy a couple and be on the safe side. Safe side! That was a joke. Unsafe side, really. Depended which way you looked at it. Nick would be sorry when he was gone. So damned superior, thinks he's God. He'll be sorry! They all would be. His grandmother (he saw her again, vitriolic, vituperative, just as she always used to be) for calling him unnatural; his mother for not letting him stay off school. Did she think he asked to stay off for no reason?

On his way home he bought two bottles of aspirin from two different chemist's. Louise was already back from work. She said, 'Are you going to come to the hospital with me to see your gran?' He supposed he might as well; it would be the last time.

'She'll be ever so pleased,' said Louise.

He doubted that.

147

His grandmother was a bit groggy, from the tests they had given her.

'When will they have the results?' said Louise.

'Tomorrow, they said. The doctor said he'd come and tell me.'

They had been there about ten minutes when Sal came in. She was all done up in fancy gear for the disco: a little red skirt that barely covered her bum, and sandals cross-gartered all the way up to her thighs. Her face grew bright crimson when she saw Christopher. They acknowledged each other, awkwardly.

'How are you?' She bent and kissed his grand-mother's lemon-coloured cheek. She managed to give the impression that she actually cared. Perhaps she did. 'I've only looked in just to say a quick hello. I'm meeting someone at eight o'clock.'

She avoided Christopher's eye. She didn't realize that he already knew all there was to know. *Hot knickers* and *going all the way*. (Would she have liked to go all the way with him? Was that what she had been waiting for?)

His grandmother, making an effort because it was Sal, said, 'So where are you off to? Anywhere exciting?'

She forked at her fringe. 'Only a disco.'

'That's exciting, isn't it? I should have thought it was. I'd have enjoyed a disco at your age. Wouldn't like it now, of course; far too noisy. Can't hear yourself speak. But perhaps you young folk don't want to hear yourselves speak?'

Sal grinned and said, 'It's not really what one goes there for.'

'No, I don't suppose it is,' said his grandmother. Was it his imagination, or did they actually exchange winks?

148

He wondered if Sal would be sorry when he had gone.

He went straight up to his room when he got back and swallowed a couple of aspirins, then in a grand gesture, three all at once, and sat back to await results. While he was waiting, he made out his will. He knew it would be invalid, because of being under age and not having any witnesses, but it pleased him to leave the bulk of his few possessions to Nick.

He left his capital, £10 in premium bonds, to Louise, and a trunk full of his childhood toys, which Louise had insisted he keep ('for future generations') to his grandmother, to play with when she became senile. He liked that touch. He reckoned she deserved it. She had regained some of her old spirit after Sal had gone, spitefully hinting that people who kept themselves aloof and thought themselves too grand to mix with ordinary folk shouldn't be surprised when their girlfriends gave them up as a bad job. 'I wouldn't have put up with it, I can tell you!'

Louise had registered a feeble protest on his behalf – 'Now, Mum! That's being naughty. That's taking advantage' – but then she had tried the pathetic bit, saying that if an old woman her age couldn't speak her mind – 'I'm not long for this earth, Lou.' She wasn't the only one.

To Sal, after much deliberation and pen-chewing, he left his cricket bat. He remembered her once bemoaning the fact that Percy's didn't play cricket, 'only mouldy old rounders'. He spent the next hour carving, and then inking in, the words 'To Sal from Chris: In Memoriam.'

By ten-thirty, when Louise called up to ask whether he wanted a cup of tea, he was still alive and seemingly well. He swallowed another three aspirins and went downstairs to take what would presumably be his last mortal gaze upon the sitting-room, with its three-piece suite covered in Draylon and its pictures of girls painted bilious green and horses with flaring nostrils galloping out of the frame.

He drank his tea (his final earthly cup) sitting with Louise in front of the television. As he stood up, he felt himself sway slightly. He didn't know whether it was really the effect of all those aspirins or whether it was wishful thinking, or perhaps the shepherd's pie and tomato soup he had eaten earlier, but he seemed to be feeling somewhat peculiar. Gravely, he kissed Louise on the cheek.

'Goodnight,' he said.

'Goodnight,' said Louise. She sounded surprised. He was not in the habit of bidding her goodnight – or of kissing her.

He walked slowly up the stairs, listening to the blood pounding in his ears. He wondered why he had bothered with two bottles when one was quite obviously going to be sufficient. He had already exceeded the stated dose. He exceeded it still further, then hid the bottle beneath his pillow, turned out the light and lay down to await death.

He woke up some time later, when the house was in darkness. The sheet was wet with perspiration; he felt very sick, and his head, when he lifted it from the pillow, was too heavy to stay upright. He fell back, panting. He hadn't thought that it would be like this. He had thought that he would slip quite peacefully and quietly away in his sleep. He hoped it wasn't going to be unpleasant.

His stomach rose up into his mouth. He forced it back down again, keeping his lips compressed. There didn't seem much point taking aspirins if all that was going to happen was that you spewed them up again. Firmly he sealed his eyes against a series of spinning red whorls. Perhaps if he were to lie very, very still and concentrate on the world to come . . .

It was difficult trying to concentrate on something which might not exist; he wasn't at all sure that he believed in life after death. He remembered Nick making him listen to *The Dream of Gerontius* for the first time. He had said, 'The words are rubbish but the music is sublime.' Had he listened to music before he became friends with Nick? He couldn't remember. Bits and pieces, maybe: the *Danse Macabre*, the *1812*, *Night on the Bare Mountain*. Nothing complicated. Nick had introduced him to practically everything he knew.

He wished he could have spoken to Nick just one more time. He ought to have responded to that poem of Sal's, as well; he never had sent her a reply. He could have sent her a poem. What could he have sent her?

He lay, with his eyes tight shut against the red whorls, going through Shakespeare sonnets in his head. *Shall I compare thee to a summer's day – When to the sessions of sweet silent thought* . . . There had to be one somewhere; you could always find what you wanted in Shakespeare. *No longer mourn for me when I am dead*; that was a good one. He couldn't remember how it went.

He reached out a hand for the light switch, blinked as the red whorls exploded, cautiously sat up and swung his legs over the side of the bed. His Shakespeare was just within reach. He sank back with it, exhausted by the effort. He wondered how quickly it would take him to die: whether he would be spared long enough to find a sonnet for Sal.

A sonnet for Sal . . . he found one for her fairly

quickly – *Farewell, thou art too dear for my possessing* – but more importantly – far more importantly – he found one for Nick . . .

Being your slave, what should I do but tend
Upon the hours and times of your desire?
I have no precious time at all to spend,
Nor services to do, till you require.
Nor dare I chide the world-without-end hour
Whilst I, my sovereign, watch the clock for you,
Nor think the bitterness of absence sour
When you have bid your servant once adieu.
Nor dare I question with my jealous thought
Where you may be, or your affairs suppose,
But like a sad slave stay and think of naught
Save where you are how happy you make those.
    So true a fool is love that, in your will
    Though you do anything, he thinks no ill.

His heart raced as he read it through. Why hadn't he thought of it sooner? A sonnet for Nick! It was the one approach that might just get through to him. God! he thought. I don't want to die!

In sudden panic he hurled himself off the bed, fell with a thump to his knees, hauled himself up, stumbled across to the door, flung it open, staggered across the landing and lurched his way downstairs to the kitchen, where like one demented he threw glass after glass of a loathsome mixture of salt and water down his throat. He then capered back up the stairs on all fours like an ape, along the passage to the bathroom. Feverishly, he flung open the door of the medicine cabinet and peered in amongst the array of pills and potions, of bottles and boxes and sachets and tubes hoarded by his grandmother. Only pausing to glance at the labels and make sure he was not adding poison to the aspirins, he helped himself to samples of everything he could find – Castor Oil and Andrew's Liver Salts, Gees' Linctus, blackcurrant cordial, Friar's Balsam, Sloan's Liniment, peppermint mouthwash. As a final measure, he leaned over the basin and stuffed his fingers as far down his throat as he could reach, with some difficulty bringing up a watery portion of shepherd's pie and tomato soup.

'Christopher?' Louise had appeared in the doorway. 'What's happening? What's the matter?'

He said, 'I suddenly remembered ... I forgot to clean my teeth before I went to bed.'

'So what are you thudding up and down the stairs for?'

'I went to get something.'

'Well, I wish you'd make a bit less noise about it ... it's two o'clock in the morning!'

They always said that two o'clock was when the body was at its lowest ebb. More people died at two o'clock than at any other time. If he could just stay alive till three he might be OK. He tried sitting up with a book, but his eyes kept closing in spite of his efforts to prevent them. He wondered, as sleep overcame him, whether death was oblivion or whether he would be able to stand back and watch it happen.

9

He awoke next morning to find himself paralysed in his upper limbs, both arms like lead appendages, dense and immovable. Terror seared like paint-stripper through his veins. So this was it! This was how it happened! The end of Christopher . . .

It took him several seconds to work out that the cause of the paralysis was the fact that he had been lying face downwards with his hands trapped beneath the pillow.

With much humping and grunting he managed to heave himself on to his side. His one arm flobbed down over the edge of the bed; the other remained where it was, beneath the pillow. His watch, his only time piece, was on the wrist of the arm that was dangling in space. He tried squinting at it over the edge of the bed, but through some quirk – an affectation from his juvenile days – he wore the watch on the inside of his wrist, cunningly hidden from view.

He fell back again, exhausted by all the gymnastics, wondering what the time was and why Louise hadn't been in to bludgeon him into wakefulness.

She came in now, dead on cue. 'Christopher, this

is the third time I've called you! Are you getting up today or aren't you?'

He said, 'I can't, my arms are paralysed.'

'What are you talking about, your arms are paralysed? Get out of that bed, for goodness' sake! It's gone midday.'

'*Midday?*' That alarmed even him. He struggled to sit up, lugging his arms with him. He had things to do.

'I'm going to see your gran after lunch. Are you coming with me?'

'I can't today.'

'She'd like to see you. She doesn't have that many visitors.'

Who was surprised? Who'd want to?

'I'll come tomorrow,' he said.

'Well, you just get yourself up and dressed. I'm going to prepare some lunch.'

He went, after lunch, into Bromley, to the bookshop where he and Nick did most of their browsing, and bought a pocket-sized edition of Shakespeare's *Sonnets*. He then bought a card from W H Smith and took it into the gardens near the Churchill Theatre to copy out his sonnet for Sal:

> *Farewell, thou art too dear for my possessing,*
> *And like enough thou know'st thy estimate.*
> *The charter of thy worth gives thee releasing;*
> *My bonds in thee are all determinate . . .*

He wrote out all fourteen lines of it, put the card in the envelope, addressed it to Hawthorn Avenue and stuck on a first-class stamp which he had filched from his grandmother's secret store which she kept in the bureau drawer beneath her pension book. He felt a sense of graciousness, almost of benevolence, as he dropped the envelope into a post-box. How much more civilized to part company by means of a poem than to scream and shout and call people names. It was Sal who had done all the name-calling, not him; he had just shut up and taken it. Considering some of the things she had said to him he reckoned he had shown great restraint. The poem was the final, finishing, sophisticated touch.

On the way back to Holt Wood in the bus he anxiously read through the sonnet he had found for Nick, checking it was as it should be. Nick would know, of course, that it was tongue in cheek, but at least it might amuse him. It was all he had to hope for.

By three o'clock he was standing at the front door of Marden, his Shakespeare *Sonnets*, marked at the appropriate page, clutched in his hand in a paper bag. He had expected the Spanish au pair to answer his ring, but instead found himself staring up at Nick's brother and was instantly thrown into confusion. Gerald was tall and dark, more beefy than Nick, more conventionally good-looking. He always made Christopher feel like some brain-damaged dwarf.

'Oh, it's you,' he said. He couldn't have made it plainer that he would have preferred it not to be. 'If you want Nick, he's up in his room, but I don't know whether –'

'I just came to give him something.' He held out the book, in its protective wrapping. He was glad he had had the forethought to keep the bag: he wouldn't want Gerald reading his private poem. 'Could you give him this, and I'd like to wait for the reply, please.'

Grudgingly, Gerald stepped back a pace, waving Christopher inside. 'You'd better go through. You know the way.'

Susan Sheringham was in the sitting-room, perched on what looked like a bar stool painting her nails with silvery pink polish.

'Hello, Christopher.' She drooped an elegant hand. 'Don't touch the nails, they're still wet ... have you come to talk to Nick? I'm not sure he's in a talking sort of mood. He's been very strange just lately, I think it's a reaction to Swiss Granny. He seems to have taken it far harder than anyone realized. I suppose he hasn't spoken to you about it?'

'Not really,' said Christopher.

'No.' She sighed, splayed a hand and blew on her nails. 'I didn't think he would. Does it strike you as pathological? Or are all teenagers like this? It must be something to do with pollution ... I never had this trouble with his brother. I'm packing them both off to the South of France next week. Let Gerald see if he can get anywhere with him. I've done my best, goodness knows. People usually find me very *easy* to talk to ... you can go up and see him if you want. I don't know if he'll let you in. Do you want to try?'

'It's all right,' said Christopher. 'I've sent him a message.'

'Oh! Well, that's one way of approaching the problem.'

'I'm just waiting for a reply.'

Mrs Sheringham laughed her tinkling laugh. 'And do you think you'll get one?' She held out a box of cigarettes. 'Smoke? No, I suppose you don't. Nasty, unhealthy habit. Come and light one for me, then you can pour me a drink. Straight Scotch. Do you want one? Or don't you drink either? God, you're so clean-living, you people!' She cupped her hand round his as clumsily he wielded the lighter. 'So, you're waiting for a reply, are you?'

'Yes,' he said.

She laughed again, as nervously he unscrewed the cap on the whisky bottle. 'What a funny pair you are! I get no end of amusement from you. I suppose I must have been the same when I was your age. And yet, I don't know ... I have the feeling I was a bit more of a *goer*. Where have I gone wrong, do you think? How did I come to produce this talented, introspective, *churned-up* teenager? Are you talented and introspective and churned-up? Or are you happy and carefree? We were all happy and carefree in my day. Just wanted a good time. Now you're all so complex and bowed down.'

He thought about Sal; she wasn't complex and bowed down. All she had ever wanted was a good time.

The Spanish au pair came in, holding his Shakespeare *Sonnets* before her as if they were a porcelain vase.

'For you,' she said. 'From Nick.'

He accepted it as calmly as he could. It was no longer in its paper bag, and there was a bookmark sticking out between the pages.

'Well?' said Mrs Sheringham. 'Aren't you going to look?'

He hadn't really wanted to do so in her presence, but it seemed there was no alternative. Trying to stop his hands from shaking he opened the sonnets at the place marked. One had been lightly ticked with a pencil. No. CXVI. He glanced through it quickly: relief was instantaneous.

Let me not to the marriage of true minds (ran Nick's sonnet)

158

Admit impediments; love is not love
Which alters when it alteration finds,
Or bends with the remover to remove.

'So?' Susan Sheringham sounded amused. 'Is it all all right, or has he taken umbrage?'

Carefully, Christopher closed the book. 'It's all right, thank you. I'll be going now.'

It was strange to feel happy again after all those weeks of misery. He marched back down the hill singing Beethoven's *Ode to Joy*, beating time with his copy of the *Sonnets*. It seemed almost indecent: as if he had just been released from a period of mourning and ought still to be suitably grieved and sober. Hard to believe that this time yesterday he had been planning to do away with himself.

He discovered Louise sitting in the front room with a damp handkerchief pressed to her face.

'What's the matter?' he said. He felt a sudden strong compulsion to be affectionate towards her: to be filial and protective. 'What's wrong?'

Louise blotted at her eyes with the handkerchief. Too late, he remembered his grandmother.

'Has something happened?' he said.

'We had the – results – of the – tests.' Louise's voice was muffled by the handkerchief. 'It's what we feared . . . she's got a tumour.'

'Oh.' He stood, stiff and awkward, wondering what to do. He ought to touch her, or something. She would probably like it if he touched her. He compromised by sitting down next to her on the sofa. 'Just because it's a tumour,' he said, 'doesn't necessarily mean it's malignant, does it?'

'At her age –' Louise's voice broke. 'They're going

to operate first thing on Monday.'

'Operate? That probably means it's going to be OK, then.' He suggested it diffidently. 'I mean, otherwise they wouldn't bother, would they? They'd just give her drugs and send her home again. I mean, they need the beds, don't they? They wouldn't bother operating if they didn't think it was going to do some good . . . well, they wouldn't, would they? Wouldn't be worth it.'

'I don't know.' Louise shook her head. She blew her nose and pushed the handkerchief up her sleeve, where it lay in a fat bulge like a misplaced bicep. 'I'm sorry to make all this fuss. It's just that, your gran . . . she's all I've got in the world. Apart from you, of course. But your gran's been almost like a mother to me.'

'Yeah. Well –' He patted her hand, in avuncular fashion. 'She'll be all right, you'll see. What can I get you? Want a cup of tea?'

'That would be lovely,' said Louise. She gave him a watery smile. 'You can be so nice when you want to be.'

IO

He found himself a job, that summer vacation, stacking the shelves in Sainsbury's. Apart from a brief spell delivering newspapers at the age of eleven, it was the first job he had ever had. The work itself was of a boredom that was mind-blowing, but he enjoyed the feeling of having money in his pocket which he had actually earned, rather than being given him by Louise.

He bought her a present at the end of the first week, a big shawl covered in multi-coloured peacocks, all reds and mauves and brilliant orange. He thought she would say it was too bright, or too big, or she didn't know how to wear it, but gratifyingly she draped it round her shoulders that same evening, when they went to the hospital to visit his grandmother.

His grandmother, not knowing where it had come from, said, 'That's a very pretty shawl you've got there, Lou.' She tried to backtrack when she discovered who had bought it. She said, 'Of course, the colours'll probably run when you wash it.'

'Oh, I don't think so,' said Louise. She was really chuffed, he could see that. He thought he would buy her a little something for each week that he worked, to make up for all the aggro he had caused her over the years.

He had bought his grandmother a bunch of flowers, which met with the usual grudging reception: roses didn't last, they dropped as soon as you cut them, she did wish people wouldn't waste their money. Louise flashed him a smile, nervous and apologetic, but he had learnt by now to bite his tongue: his grandmother, as she frequently reminded them, was 'not long for this world.' She had survived the operation, but the surgeon had told her, 'He couldn't remove the whole of the thing, I'd never have come through it.'

She repeated it to them often, seeming to take pride in it. Christopher, who would once have grown impatient, now sat thinking of sonnets in his head, nodding and ah-ing just sufficiently to keep her happy.

He needed to think of sonnets – or at any rate, quotations. He had that morning received a postcard from Nick in the South of France: *J. Caesar, IV.iii.85.* That was all it had said. On looking it up in his *Complete Works* he had read, '*A friend should bear his friend's infirmities.*' He was still trying to decide whether the infirmities in question were supposed to be his or Nick's.

He had also received another communication from Sal. It had been handed to him, in the usual surly fashion, by Glenn, who along with Pete Dossett was also employed on the shelf-stacking. He hadn't been too keen on opening Sal's letter. He didn't think she would be abusive, but she might be insulting: he didn't want any more of that '*True love hath your heart*' stuff. He found that she, too, had had recourse to Shakespeare:

That you were once unkind befriends me now –

That *he* was once unkind? She had been the one slinging all the shit!

> And for that sorrow which I then did feel
> Needs must I under my transgression bow,
> Unless my nerves were brass or hammered steel.
> For if you were by my unkindness shaken,
> (so, she admitted it)
> As I by yours, y'have passed a hell of time,
> And I, a tyrant, have no leisure taken
> To *weigh how once I suffered in your crime.*

Crime? What crime? I committed no crime, lady! He rushed that same evening to get out his *Sonnets.* The following day he sent off one to Nick – *How like a winter hath my absence been* – and one to Sal – *Say that thou didst forsake me for some fault.*

It was a game he could have played indefinitely, but the next card he had from Nick (safely enclosed in an envelope) said simply, 'Thoughts about Guy and Oliver ...' He found it reassuring. It had worried him that Nick might permanently have jettisoned Guy and Oliver. He didn't know how long Charlotte Brontë had maintained her connexion with Zamorna – he supposed, though he couldn't envisage it, that there might come a day when he had outgrown his need for an alternative persona – but he was not yet ready to face exile from the world which he and Nick had inhabited for so long.

He didn't hear from Sal again until the middle of August, when she sent him a vulgar glossy card of the *Promenade des Anglais.* In her round, firm script she wrote: *Having a wonderful time. X marks the spot. Wish you were here. Up yours. Sal.*

He said to Glenn that morning, as they were stacking tins of dog food, 'What's Sal doing in the South of France?' There was a second's pause, then Glenn said, 'Uh?' He probably couldn't believe that Christopher had spoken: they had been stacking in total silence for the past several weeks.

'I had this card from Sal – from the South of France.'

'Oh. Yeah. She's gone there. With a friend. Girl from school.'

'What, on their own?'

'Nah, with her parents. Caravan. Place called Grasse.' As an afterthought he added, 'Better than Sainsbury's.'

'You can say that again.'

That evening, he looked in his old school atlas. He found Grasse easily enough, just above Nice, to the north-west. He couldn't find the place where Nick was staying – Mont de Luciole; it was obviously too small. But in any case, it was probably nowhere near to where Sal was. And even if it were, he could hardly see Nick and Sal frequenting the same places. It disgruntled him sufficiently, however, for him to say to Louise over supper, 'Sal's gone to the South of France.'

It seemed that Louise already knew about it: Sal had told his grandmother, who had told her.

'Nobody told me,' he said.

'I didn't think you'd be interested,' said Louise.

He supposed he wasn't, really. It just irked him to think of both Sal and Nick swanning around enjoying themselves while he was stuck here stacking shelves. It had almost been better at Smeaton-on-Sea.

At the beginning of September, his grandmother died. He tried very hard to conjure up the appropriate emotions – to feel at least a vestigial sense of loss – but all he could think of was, 'Now I shan't have to bother going to the hospital any more.'

He had grown accustomed, over the past few weeks, to living without her: the sound of her voice, querulously nagging, endlessly upbraiding him for his unnaturalness, had already begun to fade. Now it was silenced for ever, leaving him neither with feelings of triumph, at a battle finally won, nor of remorse for all those past occasions of deliberate goading. Leaving him, in fact, with no feelings at all; which surely couldn't be right?

Dutifully he attended the funeral, dressed up in a dark suit bought specially for the occasion – Louise, striving to be practical even in the hour of her grief, said that it would do for 'when you go for your interviews, for university'. Did she really think that he was going to wear a *suit*? He foresaw battles in the months to come, but knew that now was not the time. Louise was weepy and inclined to burst into tears at the least provocation. Even his suggestion, intended to be helpful, that they should turn his grandmother's bedroom into a study had caused her to break down. He still didn't know what he had said that was wrong; after all, one had to be positive.

The only people to turn up at the funeral, apart from himself and Louise and a handful of his grandmother's old cronies, were the Sandersons, with Sal. Sal glanced across at Christopher and turned down the corners of her mouth in a sort of rueful half-grin; he did the same in return. She was all brown and glowing from the South of France. Her features, which had once struck him as slightly puddingy, seemed to have firmed up, revealing the bone structure. He still didn't think she could be called pretty, but he could see that she was attractive.

Afterwards, back in Dalmally Road for the statutory glasses of sherry and egg-and-cress sandwiches, she came up to him.

'Guess who I bumped into,' she said, 'while I was away?'

He knew immediately; he didn't have to guess. But obediently he played the game her way. 'Who did you bump into while you were away?'

'Your friend Nickelarse.' She brought the name out with a flourish. 'We were in this bar one evening, and he came in with his brother. He's rather dishy, isn't he? Tanya – that's the girl I was staying with – she really went for him.'

'Went for Nick?'

'No! For his brother.'

He supposed there were girls that might.

'I'm changing schools, by the way. Did I tell you? I'm going to Calder High.'

'That's a sixth form college.'

'Right.' Her eyes danced over the rim of her sherry glass. 'They still don't play cricket, but at least they're not prissy.'

Nick came back from holiday just two days before the start of the winter term. He didn't telephone Christopher from the airport because, as he later explained, Gerald was with him. They met the next morning and went into Bromley to do the rounds of Weedon's, the bookshops, the library. Things were the same as they had ever been – with one slight difference: Christopher for once had money in his pocket. It made him, perhaps, slightly more assertive when it came to the choosing of

166

records, so that he actually vetoed *Portuguese Poly-phony* and Byrd masses, sticking out, instead, for a recording of *Tosca* with Maria Callas.

'I'm sick of all that bloodless, religious muck!'

Nick registered a mild protest to the effect that *Tosca* was sadistic and immature, but backed down surprisingly quickly.

'If that's what you want,' he said.

'It is what I want.'

'OK! So have it.'

That evening, in Nick's attic domain, they resumed their role-playing as if there had never been any three-month break. It was Nick who initiated it.

'I had this thought while I was away . . . about Guy.'

Christopher settled down, obediently, cross-legged on the floor. 'Tell!'

'OK. Well –'

It seemed that for many years Guy had had an old piano teacher, whom he called 'Madame'. Madame had been teaching him since he was a child and had become, over the distance, almost as much a mother figure as a teacher. For the last few years she had been suffering from some debilitating illness – Guy was a bit vague as to what it was, but whatever it was it had severely crippled her and prevented her from any longer playing the piano. He had been in the habit of visiting her at least once every month. Now, suddenly, she was gone, and Guy was in mourning.

Despite initial hesitation, Christopher was swiftly drawn into the scenario. Oliver was full of penitence: he had not been there when Guy had heard the news of his beloved Madame's passing.

'You needed me, and I let you down!'

'It couldn't be helped.'

'It could be helped! What are friends for, if not to lend support?'

They worked their way through it, through the grief and the remorse. It was an emotionally draining, if ultimately satisfying evening. *Tosca* remained unplayed: *Portuguese Polyphony* came into its own. Nick had bought it after all; he must have suspected, that morning, what the evening was likely to bring. The unaccompanied voices, rising and falling in the 'Missa pro Defunctis', exactly suited the mood.

There was a long silence as the last notes echoed and died in the vaulted roof of the great cathedral where the recording had been made. Christopher was the first to break it. He turned, slowly, to look at Nick.

'Do you want us to play *Nimrod* for her?'

Nick nodded without speaking: it was Christopher who got up to change the record. He could never remember having done so before. Always, in the past, it had been Nick, on his home ground, who had been in charge.

Things, perhaps, were not quite the same.

Things indeed were not the same. They went back to school for the winter term and suddenly, breaking the habit of years, Nick was going out of his way to talk to people. People with whom he had not exchanged two words since very possibly the start of his time at Astley now found themselves addressed by him – addressed awkwardly, stiltedly, for Nick's tongue was not atuned to the language of his peers. Not unnaturally they were confused, at a loss how to respond. It embarrassed Christopher to see Nick, of all people, making a laughing stock of himself. It reminded him uncomfortably of his grandmother, in her final days, trying to be humble. Humility had not suited her, any more than forced bonhomie suited Nick.

Tony Forbes, well meaning, no doubt – he was, on the whole, a fairly civilized human being – came up to them one morning and said, 'I'm having a party Saturday. Round my place. Don't s'pose there's any chance you putting in an appearance?'

It was aeons since anyone had thought to invite either Nick or Christopher to a party. Christopher could hardly believe it when he heard Nick, in his new chummy guise, say, 'Sure. Why not?' Even the relatively urbane Forbes was unable to hide his amazement.

'Oh,' he said. 'Good. Great. Well – see you then!'

'Are you out of your tree?' Christopher turned on Nick, incredulous. 'Go to a *party*? On Saturday evening?'

Nick shrugged. 'It'll be something different.'

It wasn't only different, it was positively grotesque. Nick was out of his element even more, if such a thing were possible, than Christopher. Left to himself, had he only been able to screw up the courage, Christopher might at least have made a stab at joining in: Nick was patently incapable of it. He stood with a ghastly fixed grin, evidently determined to demonstrate goodwill and benevolence, to show that he was enjoying himself – and no more idea than the man in the moon how to go about it. Christopher stood at his side like a mindless stooge. Forbes at one point took pity on them – either that or got irritated at the sight of a pair of dummies ruining his party – and shunted them off elsewhere.

'Come and meet Miranda. She's my sister – she goes to Calder High. She's brought some of her buddies with her.'

Miranda was in the kitchen, tearing open packets

of nibbles and dumping them in bowls. One of the buddies she had brought with her was Sal. Forbes said, 'Miranda, meet Nick and Chris.'

'Hi,' said Miranda. She gestured, with a bag of nibbles. 'This is Sal.'

'We already know each other,' said Sal.

'Of course,' said Forbes. 'Of course you do.' He sounded suitably embarrassed. 'Well, I'll – ah – I'll leave you to it. Get back to the um –'

'Here!' Miranda shoved a couple of bowls at him. 'You can help me carry these through.'

Forbes and his sister disappeared. Nick and Christopher were left in the kitchen with Sal.

'I thought you two never came to parties,' said Sal.

'We don't,' said Christopher. 'It was his dumb idea.'

'Oh.' Sal looked at Nick, and looked away again. Nick said nothing. There was a pause.

'So how are you –'

'What –'

Another pause.

'After you!'

'I can't remember what I was going to say. What were you going to say?'

'I was only going to ask you how you were getting on at Calder High?'

'Oh – great! It's smashing. A thousand times better than Percy's.'

'Even though they don't play cricket?' He'd never given her the 'in memoriam' bat. Perhaps one of these days he would.

'I'm into long-distance running, now. Training for next year's marathon. How about you? Ever done any?'

He shook his head. He'd never been able to see the point in just running. If you were going to raise money for charity, why not do something useful while you were about it?

'It's fun,' said Sal, as if in answer to his question.

Another silence fell. Sal turned on a tap and turned it off again. Nick was no longer there.

'So where's John Newman?' said Christopher. He didn't say it to be snide; only because he couldn't think of anything else. 'I didn't see him around.'

'I haven't been out with John Newman since the end of last term. How did you know I was going with him, anyway?'

'Can't remember. I guess I must have heard it somewhere.'

Her lip curled. 'Who said men don't gossip?'

He didn't like to ask her why she had stopped going with him, or who, if anyone, she was going with now. Remembering Newman's crack about hot knickers, he would guess that he'd tried it on and had his face soundly slapped as a result. Sal wasn't a girl to take just anyone messing with her. The thought of Newman getting his come-uppance gave him profound satisfaction.

A group of people had come pushing into the kitchen in search of corkscrews and glasses.

'I'll tell you something –' Sal hissed it at him as she pushed past – 'you've got a right load of jerks at that school of yours!'

He was with her on that one. He turned, and made his way back to the sitting-room in search of Nick. He found him standing by himself with a glass in his hand.

'What are you drinking?'

'Wine.'

'Wine?' In all the years he had known Nick, he

171

had never known him touch alcohol. Nick arched an eyebrow.

'You have some kind of objection?'

'I didn't think you did, that's all.'

'Why shouldn't I? Other people do.'

Other people did a whole lot of things. He didn't know why it should bother him, Nick drinking a glass of wine, but it did.

'I reckon I've had enough of this party,' he said. He had just seen Sal go up to a group of people he didn't know, presumably from Calder High. Amongst them was a blond youth with long hair tied in a pony-tail. He didn't like the way Sal was pressing up against him. 'Do you want to go?'

If Nick had elected to stay, he would almost certainly have stayed with him; but Nick seemed only too relieved that Christopher had been the one to make the first move. He said, 'Oh, if you must,' with a show of being dragged prematurely away, but made no attempt at finishing off the wine that was still in his glass.

They went back to Marden and spent the rest of the evening listening to music and role-playing Guy and Oliver agonizing over whether they should attend a party which might or might not further Guy's career. Oliver, tentatively, advanced the thesis that if a career could only be won at the expense of extreme emotional trauma then possibly it was not worth pursuing: Guy wondered again about the priesthood. They discussed whether the latter was merely a flight from reality, and Guy, finally, pushed into a corner, admitted that it could be – but if that were so, then 'Where does it leave one?'

Oliver said, 'Back where one has always been? In isolation?'

'Like social lepers.'

'It's something that creative people just have to put up with.'

'Not all creative people.'

'Some; quite a lot, I should say. In any case, it's bearable so long as there are two of you. It's when you're on your own –'

'It makes no difference! No difference! Two, one, half a dozen . . . deep down inside –'

'What?'

'*Deep down inside* . . .'

Oliver waited.

'Tendrils reach
Into the void
And the green shoots wither
For lack of nourishment.
The food that feeds the rest
Is not for them.
Slowly they die;
And with each small death goes part of the whole.'

There was a silence.

'What's that?'

'*Requiem for a Soul.*'

'By whom?'

'By me!' Nick jumped to his feet. 'What do you want next? Your blasted *Tosca*?'

*

On Monday, at school, during first break, they were doing their usual circuit of the grounds when something leapt on them from behind: it was the fool, MacMaster.

'Hi, there, you guys!' He inserted himself between them, draping his arms about their shoulders. Nick

173

visibly flinched, but did not actually disengage. 'I've come to ask a favour of you ... I want you to help me out. The both of yous. It's a little question of the Christmas revue ... I need contributions. Sketches; all kinds. Musical, satirical, just plain funny. Can I rely on you, would you say, to come up with something?'

There was a pause; then Nick said, 'How many do you want?'

'Just as many as you can manage! We need them as soon as possible – like yesterday, for preference. Or if you can't manage that, then in the next couple of weeks. We were going to do a musical, but it's fallen through, unfortunately. Now we're having to think on our feet. Mr Marriner was telling me, if it's someone to turn out sketches you're after –' his hand closed over Christopher's shoulder – 'Chris Seymour's your man. And I've worked with Nick already, of course. I'm aware of what he can do, when he sets his mind to it. So, how about it?' The hand squeezed again: all mates together. 'Can I look to you for something?'

'We'll see what we can come up with,' said Nick.

'Good man!' MacMaster dropped his hand and danced in front of them like some little squat leprechaun, one thumb stuck up by way of approval. 'I knew you'd not let me down!'

MacMaster turned, and sprinted off across the playing field.

'Dumb shit,' said Nick.

'So if he's a dumb shit what d'you want to go and promise our services for?' Christopher almost yelped it. 'Seems to me you're the dumb shit!'

'A few sketches? We can toss them off in an evening.'

'That's what you think! It's not that simple. You've got to get ideas, for a start.'

174

'We'll get ideas . . . stop being such a misery! It could be fun.'

Christopher walked on, frowning. 'I suppose Bogey hasn't been getting at you again, by any chance?'

'Bogey? No. Why?'

'All this sudden *compliance*.' This sudden craven desire to mingle and merge and be one with the crowd. It was well enough known to Christopher, but not what he expected from Nick. It made him feel as if one of the bulwarks against which he was accustomed to lean was beginning to topple.

'I've never seen any point,' said Nick, 'in cutting off one's nose to spite one's face.'

'Well! That's original! What's it supposed to mean?'

'It means you have to put up at least a token show of going along with them . . . they're the ones with the power, not us. When you've got where you want, then you can afford to give 'em the two fingers. Until that time, it's a question of learning to live with it.'

He had never thought to hear such a sentiment coming from Nick. Things were definitely not the same as they had been.

It was months since the two of them had worked on anything together. All the old projects – the *Book of Great British Turds*, the *Titillating Tales* – had long since been shelved and forgotten.

'What we need,' said Nick, 'is a long weekend . . . if we could work from Friday evening right through to Sunday we could probably crack it. How about coming over to my place?'

'What, you mean stay over?'

He and Nick had never spent the night with each other. Girls, he knew, because Sal had told him, did it all the time. She had had this girlfriend in Australia, Rachel-Anne, whom it seemed she had actually shared a bed with.

'We used to lie awake half the night just laughing and talking.'

He couldn't imagine doing that with Nick.

Louise, when he put the idea to her, became strange and aggressive.

'The whole weekend? *Sleeping* there?'

'Yes; so we can work on these sketches.'

'I don't see why there's any need for you to sleep there.'

'It means we can get more done – carry on right through the night if we feel like it. It saves having to break off.'

'I shouldn't think his parents would be too happy, being kept awake by you thumping and banging.'

'We're not going to thump and bang, and even if we were they wouldn't hear us . . . Nick's got his own suite of rooms at the top of the house. It's almost like a separate flat.'

Louise scrunched her lips. 'I'd rather you didn't. I don't like the idea of you being away all weekend.'

'It's only two days!'

'Yes, and it's only three and a bit weeks since your gran died . . . less than a month, that's all it is!'

He didn't see what his grandmother had to do with it.

'I need time,' said Louise. 'I know it didn't mean anything to you, but –'

'Yes, it did,' he said. 'Of course it did.'

He was having a serious campaign for being kinder to Louise, inaugurated on the day of his grandmother's funeral, when it had occurred to him, with a heavy sense of responsibility, that he was now the only person she had left in the world. It was the first funeral he had ever been to. Louise had wept and he had stood there, with three old women dressed in black, together with Sal and her parents, trying desperately to feel something, to force himself to feel something, and nothing had come, and he had felt ashamed of himself. Surely one ought to feel at least a passing emotion on the death of one's grandparent? Nick had; but then Swiss Granny hadn't spent the whole of his life telling him he was unnatural.

'I know it's awful for you,' he said, as tactfully as he could, though he did think that by now she ought to be starting to get over it. 'I mean, I know I can't feel it the same as you, but you're always on at me to get out and do things, and now when I'm trying to —'

'That's not getting out and doing things!' she cried. 'That's only going round to Nick's! You're always going round there — you practically live there!'

Jealousy? he thought. Could his own mother possibly be jealous of his friendship with Nick?

'I only go round there once a week,' he said.

'Once a week every week! For goodness knows how many years! Ever since you started at that wretched school!'

He was nettled. 'I didn't choose to go to Astley! You were the one that put me in for it.'

'That was —' She stopped.

'What?'

'That was your gran. She wanted it.'

'So why go on at me about it?'

'I'm not going on at you.' Wearily, Louise pushed a lock of greying hair off her temples. 'I just wish you could have found some friend other than Nick!'

'You hate him,' he said, 'don't you?'

'Of course I don't hate him! That's a terrible thing

to say. If anything, I feel sorry for him. What kind of a life has he had, shut away all by himself at the top of that great mausoleum of a place? It's no wonder he's –' she waved a hand – 'as he is.'

'How is he?' said Christopher.

'Oh! I don't know! Odd – different. It's like talking to a robot. You never feel you're making contact.'

'That's only because you don't know him properly.'

'Well, maybe it is, but I still think it's a great shame you broke with Sarah. You were getting on so nicely. I've always felt *that* had something to do with Nick.'

'What, us getting on so nicely?'

'No! Breaking up. I've felt he's been a bad influence over you – you're so easily led, he's like some kind of – of Svengali, or something.'

'Sven *what*?'

'Svengali!' Louise snapped it, almost hysterically.

'What's a Sv–'

'Oh, don't be stupid! You know perfectly well what I mean! Some kind of evil genius.'

'Nick's not a genius. His IQ isn't any higher than mine.'

'Christopher –' Louise checked herself. 'Oh, do whatever you want to do! It's not worth arguing with you.'

'So is it OK? If I just go round there this weekend?'

'I told you,' she said. 'Do what you want to do. I can't be bothered arguing with you any more.'

I I

The Spanish au pair had departed from Marden and the Sheringham household had been thrown into temporary confusion.

'We'll have to get our own meals,' said Nick. 'Can you cook?'

He had never given much thought to the matter. His grandmother had accused him of not even knowing how to make a cup of tea, which was totally untrue. What *was* true, however, was that he had not the faintest idea how long it took to boil an egg. Neither, as it turned out, had Nick.

'What does one do to them? Just put them in a pan?'

'Put 'em in a pan and boil the shit out of 'em.'

'Yeah, but for how long?'

'Till they're like bullets.'

'But how does one know?'

Neither of them could think how one knew. Christopher hazarded a guess that possibly they might sound different when tapped with a spoon. Nick thought maybe you had to boil them till all the water had gone. They decided, in the end, to play safe and opt for baked beans instead.

'On toast,' said Nick. Even Nick knew how to do toast: you just put the bread in the toaster and pressed the button. 'Better than risking salmonella.'

'Salla monella . . . that's what my grandmother used to call it.' *You make sure those eggs are done properly, Lou, they'll give us all salla monella.*

'You could write a sketch about a girl called Salla Monella.'

'Salla Monella and her friend Liz Teria.'

They spent the whole of Friday evening tossing around ideas for sketches, trying them out on Nick's tape machine. They had the house to themselves. Gerald was up in town and not expected until late Saturday, Nick's father was abroad at a conference, his mother at the golf club, from which she had still not returned when they went to bed at twelve-thirty.

Some time in the small hours, Christopher, sleeping in the guest bedroom on the first floor, was woken by the sound of car tyres scrunching over gravel. He went across to the window to look and saw Susan Sheringham clambering from the front passenger seat of a Jag. She seemed to be having difficulty co-ordinating her movements. Whoever was in the car leaned across to slam the door behind her and the Jag shot forward out of the drive. He watched from behind the curtains as Nick's mother stood fumbling in the light of a street lamp for her key, then lurched unsteadily, right arm poked forward, key presumably in hand, towards the porch. He tried to imagine Louise coming home plastered at two o'clock in the morning but the picture refused to gel. He supposed on the whole he was pretty glad. Once a year, perhaps, when they all got sloshed at the Christmas do, it might be amusing, but he didn't think that he would care for it to be a regular occurrence.

He wondered if he were being prudish, and what Sal would say. It wasn't really something which he could discuss with Nick.

Next morning, they were alone in the kitchen: his mother, Nick said, rarely emerged before midday. They cooked more toast and Christopher made tea, somewhat experimentally as the tea came out of a caddy instead of tea-bags from a packet and he wasn't sure how many spoonfuls to use. Nick was vague on the subject and could only suggest 'the same as tea-bags', so he put in two spoons and the result was rather like drinking washing-up liquid diluted with hot water.

'Does it always taste like this?' he said.

Nick shrugged. 'I guess so.'

Nick wasn't really terribly interested in food and drink. Even as a kid, back in the first form, he had never spent any of his pocket money on the sickly delicacies which had tempted Christopher. Odd, for a person who had spent all his summer holidays on the Continent; you'd have thought he would have been a bit of a gourmet.

After breakfast they went into Bromley, as usual. In Weedon's, on their way down to the basement, they passed Sal picking over a rack of Top 20 CDs. She was with the blond pony-tailed youth from Forbes' party. Fortunately she had her back towards them and they managed to get past without being spotted. Neither of them said anything. Christopher pretended to himself that he hadn't noticed her; maybe Nick quite genuinely hadn't. By the time they came back up the stairs she had gone.

They took sandwiches home with them to save having to cook more toast. Susan Sheringham was wandering the house in a red silk dressing-gown. She looked somewhat raddled in the cold light of day; he thought perhaps she wasn't wearing any make-up. Louise never wore any and so always looked raddled, but he was used to Nick's mother with plenty of colour.

'What have you got there?' she said. 'Oh, sandwiches! How clever of you!'

'Did you want some?' said Nick.

'No, sweetie, I couldn't; not at this time of day. But it's a kind thought.' She fished a packet of cigarettes from her pocket. 'So what are you two up to?'

'Working.'

'My dear! How industrious! Is it something frightfully important?'

'Not really,' said Nick. 'Only the end-of-term revue.' He picked up a box of matches and lit one for her. 'We're doing some sketches.'

'What fun! Are they madly witty and satirical?'

'I doubt it,' said Nick.

'We haven't actually written them yet,' said Christopher. 'They might just turn out to be rather puerile.'

Susan Sheringham laughed her silvery laugh, at the back of which was a smoker's rattle. It occurred to Christopher that she would make a good heroine for *La Dame aux Camélias*; she had the same worn, fragile quality.

'Well, don't work too hard, you know what they say ... all work and no play makes Nicholas and Christopher two very dull little boys. I shall be up at the club all evening, why don't you come and join me? Give yourselves a break.' She looked at Christopher. 'You're very welcome.'

Christopher made an inarticulate mumbling sound. Nick said, 'It depends how much we manage to get done.'

'Oh, don't be such a slave driver! Let your hair down for once and enjoy yourselves!'

'I wouldn't want to embarrass you,' said Nick, 'in front of your friends.'

'Darling, you couldn't embarrass me if you tried! You might have done once, when you were a snotty-nosed brat; but you're a big boy now, and you've become quite presentable . . . I might almost feel proud to be seen with you.' She closed an eye at Christopher. 'See what you can do,' she said. 'Take him out of himself!'

Christopher grinned, feebly. They collected a couple of Cokes and retired to the attic with their sandwiches.

'Just for the record,' said Nick, 'I have no desire to be *taken out of myself*. I'm quite happy the way I am.'

Christopher wondered, for the first time, if that were actually true. Did Nick really not care that people whispered and talked? Did it genuinely not bother him, this sense of isolation?

'She nurtures the belief,' said Nick, 'that we all ought to be out there, merging and mingling and losing ourselves in the mob.'

Nick had tried doing just that. He had insisted on going to the party and of course it hadn't worked out; Christopher could have told him it wouldn't. But why had he gone there in the first place?

'Don't worry,' Christopher said. 'Mine's just the same. Nagging all the time . . . get out and *do* things. At least there's an excuse for yours: she *does* get out and do things. Mine never does anything at all. Just sits indoors watching television every night. Then she goes on at *me*. Why people can't just leave people alone to do their own thing . . . they all think we're raving mad, of course; you know that. Don't you? You know they think we're raving potty? Just because we don't do the same things they do. Because we don't *go with the herd.* I never told you, did I, last term, that week you were away –'

'Not now,' said Nick. 'Grab a sandwich and let's get on with things.'

'I just w–'

'Some other time. I'm going to switch the tape on. Then we can listen to what we did last night. Decide if any of it's worth keeping.'

It wasn't any use trying to make Nick talk about things he didn't want to talk about; he had tried before and failed. Resigned, he picked up a cheese and pickle sandwich and settled down to the serious business of being witty and amusing.

They worked through without a break. Gratifyingly, much of the stuff which had convulsed them the previous evening – the Judge Shoot, the Flasher on the Rocks, the Pet Jelly sketch – still amused on second hearing. It was a question, in most cases, of shaping and polishing. At eight o'clock they ventured forth, ravenous, to forage for food.

'Toast?' said Nick.

'Toast and what?'

'Find something.'

He found a tin of pilchards in tomato sauce, a tin of asparagus tips and a tin of guavas. On the kitchen table was a note from Susan Sheringham: *Darlings, Don't work too hard, come down to the club about 10 o'c., why not? Champagne in fridge if you feel like a celebration. Have fun!*

After eating their pilchards and asparagus tips, followed by the tin of guavas, they separated – Nick going off to work out some musical accompaniments on the piano, Christopher to finish off a monologue delivered by the long-suffering wife of a do-it-yourself maniac who had converted his house into a version of Spaghetti Junction.

You'll get yourself run over one of these days, that's what you'll do! If you must keep a set of traffic lights outside the kitchen door you might at least take the trouble to watch what colour they're showing . . . I don't want any more accidents like the one you had last week when you decided to go one-way across the living-room. One-way, indeed! As if it's not bad enough already, what with bollards all over the lobby and roundabouts at the foot of the stairs and no-waiting signs right in front of the telephone . . . the next step'll be parking meters by the umbrella stand, I shouldn't wonder, and then what do we do every time it starts raining?

The monologue lasted a good five minutes. He envisaged it being spoken by someone resembling his grandmother, grumbling on as she performed some household chore – the ironing, say, or the washing-up. He wondered who would be capable of taking the part. The way he had read it into the tape was exactly the way he wanted it to be, but he knew it would never occur to MacMaster to suggest he might do it. There had been a time, a long time ago, when he had quite fancied himself as a performer. He had once played a frog in a primary school production, and in his first year at Astley – the memory suddenly leaped back at him – he had been praised for his portrayal of Puck in a junior school version of *A Midsummer Night's Dream*. It had been written up in the school magazine. There had been a photograph of him – *Christopher Seymour as Puck*. He couldn't now remember what the write-up had said, but he knew it had been good. Louise had cut it out and put it somewhere. He had a sudden urge to read it again.

Nick burst in, waving some sheets of manuscript paper. 'That's it! I've done! Let's get it all on tape, so we can run it in the morning.'

It took them until well past midnight to record everything; by then they were on a definite high. There was something about the act of creation, albeit only a few crummy sketches for MacMaster, which sent the adrenalin racing. Even Nick, the self-contained, came close to spontaneous madness.

'Mahler! This demands Mahler!'

Mahler's Second, in all its exultant glory, poured forth from the attics, filling the house with an ecstasy of sound. The floorboards shook as the bass rolled and thundered, Mahlerian brass baying down the stairwell.

'Go for it, Mahler baby!'

They came, reluctantly, to their senses with the angry pounding of footsteps up the attic stairs.

'For God's sake!' It was Gerald, red-faced and apopleptic. 'I could hear that racket half a mile away!'

'Sorry,' said Nick. 'I'll turn it down.'

'Turn it down? You can damn well turn it off! Do you know what the time is? It's gone two o'clock!' He glared at Christopher. 'Your mother will be out of her mind!'

'It's all right, he's staying the night,' said Nick.

'Oh. Is he? Well. OK! But just shut the racket!'

'It's not a racket, it's Mahler's Second.'

'I don't care what it is! Shut it. It's time you were both in bed anyway.'

They didn't have to go to bed just because Gerald said so. They stayed up another twenty minutes, as a matter of principle, but the mood had been broken, and in any case Mahler's emotional orgies could not be enjoyed at half blast.

It was diabolical, thought Christopher, the way people took it upon themselves to go round ruining other people's pleasures. What harm had they been doing, just listening to music?

He had been in bed only about five minutes, still too wide awake to settle down, when the door opened and Nick appeared.

'Put the light on, I've got something for us.'

'What? W—'

'SH! Don't wake old misery-guts, he's right underneath . . . here!' He thrust a bottle into Christopher's hand.

'What's this?'

'Champagne.'

'*Champagne?*'

'For celebrating. Come on!' Nick set a couple of glasses on the table. 'Get it opened, I've got another one here.'

Christopher stared, dubiously, at the foil-covered top. He had never opened a bottle of champagne before – he had never even *seen* a bottle of champagne before, other than on the shelves at Sainsbury's.

'Do you think we ought?'

'Of course we ought! That's what she left it for, isn't it? *Champagne in fridge, in case you feel like celebrating* . . . So! I feel like celebrating. Pop the cork and let's get on with it. Oh, give it here! I'll do it!'

Champagne, thought Christopher, was a very misleading beverage. Like a kind of upper-crust joke on the lumpen proles, splashing out their life savings getting it for weddings and for anniversaries, then tossing it back like it was nothing more than fizzy lemonade

187

and reckoning they'd been had because what was so special about it anyway? Famous last words. What was so special about it was that it was one of those drinks that was about a thousand times more alcoholic than it tasted.

He didn't realize this at the time, it was something he only discovered when it was already far too late to do anything about it. Possibly Nick didn't realize either, for although not a prole like Christopher, Nick wasn't in the habit of imbibing.

They rolled about Christopher's bed, propped on their elbows beneath the duvet, glasses in hand, hiccuping and giggling and whispering like first-formers, like Sal with Rachel-Anne.

'Less 'ave a judge shoot! Break open 'nother boxer judges.'

'Where's me gun, Carruthers? Hand me me gun!'

'Got the bastard!'

'Oops, sorry your judgeship!'

Helpless with laughter, they fell back against the pillows.

'How about the old flasher on the rocks, then? Luring all them poor little sailor boys to their doom –'

'Don't do that, sailor, you'll go blind!'

Ho ho ho. Ha ha ha.

'What –' Christopher spoke between gasps – 'what d'you think old Paddy MacMaster'll make of it?'

'Never mind MacMaster! What about Bogey?'

'His lads . . . even *knowing* about such things –'

'What we need is some really seedy character, in a dirty raincoat.'

'Harry Morgan.'

They collapsed, sobbing. One of the empty champagne bottles, left unregarded in the middle of the duvet, fell to the floor with a thunk. They were too far gone to care.

'Harry Morgan –'

'Playing with his organ –'

'God! What a sight!'

Without any warning, the door suddenly crashed open. Gerald stood there, face mottled. 'What's going on in here?'

Their laughter ceased abruptly; they struggled, drunkenly, to sit up. Christopher felt consumed with guilt, and wondered why. There was no reason for guilt, the champagne had been left for them, it had been theirs to drink as they wished; why didn't Nick say so?

Gerald bent to pick up the empty bottle. 'You make me sick,' he said. 'The pair of you . . . it's no more than I suspected, but you still make me sick! I've been right about you all along . . . you're disgusting! The pair of you. Totally bloody disgusting!' He jerked his head at Nick. 'Get back to your own room – and another time at least have the decency to conduct your sordid perversions under someone else's roof . . . this happens to be my parents' home.'

Nick went off so meekly; no protest, none of his usual arrogance; he just went.

'As for you –' Gerald looked contemptuously at Christopher. 'You make me sick.'

Next morning, when he awoke, Christopher sensed at once that it was late. He looked at his watch and it said quarter-past eleven. He had no idea what time it had been when Gerald had come bursting in on their drunken revelry. The champagne bottles had gone, but the two glasses, one half-full of flat champagne, still stood witness on the bedside table.

189

Slowly he dressed and went out on to the landing. Silence; then faintly, from downstairs, the muted murmur of voices. He tiptoed to the banisters and listened, trying to make out whether the male voice belonged to Gerald or to Nick. It was impossible to say, they sounded too alike.

He turned and walked back along the passage to the attic stairs to see if Nick were up yet. He would have been reluctant in any case to venture forth without him; the events of last night only made him more so.

Marden had two attic rooms divided by a short passage. One served as Nick's bedroom, the other as a sitting-room. Both were empty.

He went back down to the first landing, used the lavatory and crossed to the bathroom to wash his hands. The bathroom was locked. He started to say, 'N—' and stopped himself just in time: it could be Gerald in there.

There was a washbasin on the ground floor, in the little cloakroom tucked away behind the stairs. To reach it he had to walk past the breakfast room, the door to which was not quite shut. As he approached it, padding softly on the parquet floor in stockinged feet (he always took off his trainers because they squeaked) he heard Susan Sheringham's voice, low and impatient: 'Oh, for God's sake, Gerald! Don't be such a bigotted little blimp! All this fuss about a bit of slap and tickle ... it's hardly the end of the world.'

Christopher stood, transfixed, on the other side of the door. He heard Gerald's voice, furiously hissing in reply: 'It may not be the end of the world, but it's hardly what you would call desirable!'

'It obviously is to him; I'm afraid we can't all be the

same. I'm sure you'd like him to be a clone of you and your father –'

'I'd sooner he was a clone than a flaming pansy!'

'God, you're so self-righteous! What did I do to get lumbered with a prig for a son?'

'One prig and one pansy –'

'Yes, and I know which I prefer!'

Sounds of movement came from within the breakfast room; sounds of a chair being scraped back. Christopher turned and fled. Locked inside the downstairs cloakroom he hung out the hand-washing as long as possible in the hope that by the time he emerged Nick might have put in an appearance, but he heard no footsteps descending the stairs and as he opened the door Susan Sheringham walked past on her way from the kitchen with a pot full of coffee. She said, 'Hello, Christopher! Just in time, I've just made a fresh pot. Where's that lazy son of mine? Not up yet?'

'I think he's still in the bathroom.'

'Oh, so at least he's out of bed, that's something. Come and sit down and have some breakfast. I'm afraid there's not a lot on offer . . . toast, cereal –'

He helped himself to some cereal. Gerald picked up the Sunday newspaper and disappeared from sight. Susan Sheringham chattered gaily.

'So you managed the champagne, after all. I'm glad about that. I do find these puritanical streaks in modern youth extremely tiresome . . . a bottle of champagne never hurt anyone. I always look upon it as a sort of superior fruit salts – wonderful for a clear-out! I'm sorry I can't offer you a proper breakfast but Nick probably told you, Mercedes has left us in the lurch . . . How did you get on yesterday? Did you manage to cook yourselves anything? You obviously got a nice lot of work done. I was expecting you down at the golf club. I said, when you didn't come, I said, they'll be working and they'll have forgotten the time –'

Her voice bubbled on, bright and urgent across the breakfast table, not waiting for replies. He knew why she was doing it; she was embarrassed in case he might have heard what she and Gerald had been talking about. He wanted desperately to interrupt, to tear the camouflage away from Gerald's stupid face, to shout at him that he had got it wrong, it wasn't like that, '*We're* not like that! We were just being happy, we were excited, we were *celebrating*!'

He didn't, because there was never really any opportunity. Also because he was too much of a coward. Also because Gerald probably wouldn't believe him. Also because, when all was said and done, this was Nick's territory and these were Nick's people and it was up to Nick to set the record straight.

'Where *is* Nick?' said Mrs Sheringham. 'You don't suppose he's got a hangover and gone crawling back to bed, do you? Do you want to go and see? Tell him, if he has, the best thing for it is fresh orange juice.'

'The best thing for it –' Gerald's voice spoke sourly from behind the Sunday paper – 'is to stick to fresh orange juice in the first place.'

'Oh, pish!' Susan Sheringham picked up a piece of toast and lobbed it at him across the table. 'Don't be such a killjoy!'

Christopher wondered, as he left the room, whether it would be better for him to go straight home. He thought that it probably would. He would just check on Nick, then grab his things and go. That would leave Nick a free hand to clear the air between himself and Gerald. They could always get together next Saturday to do any final revisions on the sketches. MacMaster had given them a fortnight.

Nick's bedroom was still empty. He tried the bathroom again, but the door was still locked. He said, 'Nick?' and rattled the handle. 'You in there?' He couldn't hear any sounds of running water, or of anyone throwing up. 'Nick?' he said. 'You OK?'

There was no reply. He leaped back down the stairs and into the breakfast room, where it seemed there was yet another altercation going on.

'So!' Mrs Sheringham reached with thin, veined hand for the coffee pot. 'How is he?'

'He's still in the bathroom.'

'*Still?* What's he doing in there? Practising to swim the Channel?'

'I don't know,' said Christopher. 'He doesn't answer.'

Susan Sheringham banged down the coffee pot. Gerald tossed aside his newspaper. They left the room together, but it was Gerald who was first up the stairs, and Gerald who set his shoulder to the bathroom door.

Gerald, too, who was the first to enter.

'Nick!' he yelled. 'You bloody fool!'

Susan Sheringham covered her face with her hands. 'Oh, dear God . . .'

'Should I ring for an ambulance?' said Christopher.

Nobody answered him.

12

When Nick had recovered, they sent him abroad. Abroad seemed to be the panacea for all ills in the Sheringham family, for everything from emotional breakdown (which was what they were calling it) to impending alcoholism: Susan Sheringham had likewise been despatched, ostensibly in the role of keeper, though Louise, via an informant in the kitchens of the Merrie Kettle, had heard otherwise. A woman called Agnes, whose sister was married to the Marden odd-job man, had it on authority that Susan Sheringham had been sent away to dry out: she was to keep an eye on Nick and he was to keep an eye on her. Christopher couldn't see the arrangement working; not unless either Nick or his mother had undergone a transformation. Maybe they had. He wouldn't know. He had not been allowed to visit Nick in hospital, or even communicate with him by letter. His father had sent a stiff little note to Louise saying that 'in the circumstances' he would prefer it if 'your son had no further contact with mine'.

Louise, who at that stage had known nothing of the events which had taken place, had not unnaturally been thrown into panic.

'What circumstances? Christopher, what's happened? You're keeping something from me!'

He was forced in the end to tell her about Nick in the bathroom, in the bath full of cold water, behind the locked door. She was sufficiently shocked not to pursue the question of what had driven him to it. Christopher knew he could never have brought himself to relay Gerald's discovery of him and Nick, pissed out of their minds beneath the duvet: he couldn't be sure that she wouldn't jump to the same unwarranted conclusion. She had been uneasy about his friendship with Nick for too long. He had always thought it was a form of jealousy, because of feeling herself excluded; he wondered now whether it might not have been something else.

When finally, pushed by the cold and ominous *in the circumstances*, he was forced into telling her what Nick had attempted, he was surprised not only by the strength of her reaction but by the quality. He had braced himself for pursed lips and the claim, 'I always knew that boy was unbalanced.' He had misjudged her.

'Christopher! That's appalling!' She held out her arms as if to embrace him. For just a moment he was almost tempted to fling himself into them, but habit, ultimately, proved too strong. 'That poor boy! What he must have gone through and no one ever bothering to notice – and not one person that he felt he could turn to. Not one single one! Christopher –' She caught at his hand. 'If ever you felt like that, you would come to me, wouldn't you? Promise me that you would! Because whatever it was – I mean, whatever the reason – I would always listen to you. I would always do my very best to understand. Even if it were – well! Something you found it difficult to talk about.'

He looked at her steadily. She blushed.

'All I'm trying to say is, I'm always here if you want me. If Nick had only been able to talk to someone he might not have done – what he did. I couldn't bear the thought –'

'Don't worry,' he said. 'I'm too much of a coward.'

'I hope you don't think –' a sudden note of warning entered her voice; caused, he thought, more by anxiety than disapproval – 'I hope you don't think that what Nick tried to do had anything heroic attached to it. It was appalling and terrible and I'm desperately sorry for him, but there's nothing *brave* about it.'

That was a matter of opinion, he thought. All he knew was that he couldn't have done it. He hadn't even been able to swallow a few aspirins without flying into a panic and vomiting them back up again.

'In any case,' said Louise, 'I thought he was a Catholic? Surely for them it's a mortal sin?'

It was an aspect that hadn't occurred to him. It presumably hadn't occurred to Nick, either; or if it had, then in his misery he had dismissed it as of no significance. It choked him, the thought of Nick being that miserable and him not knowing. Nick had been his anchor point. He had always felt that here at least was *one* person able to rise above it all. Christopher might worry himself sick about the image he presented, the way they all whispered and sniggered: Nick had seemed so gloriously and genuinely immune to the petty murmurings of the world.

In the past he would have taken the new experience and used it for Guy and Oliver. He would have built a scenario, ready for role-playing when Nick had come back. Now he didn't know whether Nick ever would be coming back, for outside Marden, so Louise's spy reported, there was a big FOR SALE notice. As for Guy and Oliver, in this his hour of deepest need he found they had deserted him. Try as he might he could no longer conjure up their images nor hear them talking. For years they had been his constant companions. He had been accustomed, every night, to select a scene – an old one, many times played and replayed, or a new one, still in process of creation – and act it out in the comfort and security of bed. Most of the acting had been silent, taking place in his head, but in more intense moments he would mouth whole conversations to himself under cover of the duvet. Likewise in the morning, during that first half-hour of semi-wakefulness when all manner of extravagances became possible; that, perhaps, had been the best time of all for entering his inner world. Now, abruptly, he had no inner world, and its loss left a vacuum which ached like an empty grave.

He waited in vain for word from Nick. For a letter, for a postcard. Nothing came. Christopher had no means of communication. He guessed that any letters he tried sending would be opened and ignominiously returned to him, or even destroyed; and knew, even if he could bring himself to telephone, that no one was going to trust him with an address. He had no idea even which continent Nick was on: the spy in the kitchen only knew that it was 'abroad'. But there was no reason Nick should not write to him. Susan Sheringham had not been hostile; she had defended them, even while believing Gerald's distorted version of the truth. She would have had no objection to Nick keeping in touch. Unless, of course, they had got to her, the two of them; Nick's father and Gerald. She might not have been strong enough to withstand a joint attack, especially with the problem of her own which she already had. They had probably got on at her about that, as well.

He wondered whether he would ever hear from or see Nick again.

School, which should have been intolerable, scarcely made any impression on the yawning chasm of his consciousness. He went in, went to classes, went back home. He supposed that each day must in some subtle way be different from the one which had preceded it, but if so he no longer noticed. People must have been told that Nick was ill, for in twos and threes, these same people who once had whispered in corners now came up and awkwardly muttered at him. He gathered, from the things they muttered, and the way they muttered them, that Nick's absence had been explained in terms of a mental rather than a physical affliction. It obviously embarrassed them. It would have embarrassed him, once; now he was too numb to care.

Saturdays were the worst; they had always been a problem when Nick wasn't there, but at least in the past he had known that the absence was purely a temporary one. Now it was permanent and it was as if part of him had died. He went into Bromley and had to come out again. He kept seeing the ghosts of himself and Nick doing all those normal Saturday things which they would almost certainly never do again. In the evening he sat with Louise and watched television. He couldn't face the prospect of going up to his room and listening to music. Music had been part of his life with Nick: he couldn't imagine it without him.

In Holt Wood, on his way back from school one afternoon, he bumped into Sal. She was with a couple of girls and the blond youth with the pony-tail, but immediately detached herself on seeing Christopher.

'Sorry to hear about Nick,' she said. 'Your mum told us . . . I'm really sorry.'

Louise had told them? About Nick? He felt a dull sense of betrayal: it was his grandmother all over again. Thickly he said, 'What exactly did she tell you?'

'Well – you know!' Sal, too, was embarrassed. 'Just that he'd been kind of . . . overdoing things.'

That was a polite way of saying that someone had had a nervous breakdown. He really didn't see why Louise should have felt the need to tell the Sanderson family anything at all, but at least she had not committed the ultimate betrayal. He saw now how word had got round at school. He had wondered who had been responsible for it; he couldn't see Bogey spreading it abroad.

'How's he doing?' said Sal. 'Is he OK?'

He made noises. He couldn't bring himself to confess that he had been barred from all attempts at communication. He still burned, even now, when he thought of that jibe of hers. *Your true love hath your heart . . .* She was as bad as the rest of them; they had minds like Sunday tabloids.

'Of course, he's the type,' said Sal, 'isn't he? People like you and me, we tend to splurge. It might be a bit of a pain for other people, having to put up with us, but at least it gets it out of the system. Poor old Nick was really locked in, wasn't he?'

He didn't like the way she referred to him as 'poor old Nick' – and what did she know about him, anyway, other than what he had told her?

'I remember, when I met him that time in the South of France –' She stopped.

'That was after his grandmother had just died.'

'Yes; that's true.' She forked at her fringe. 'So how's the snob school?'

199

He humped a shoulder. 'Same as always.' He wondered what she had been going to say about the South of France.

'It must be really strange, without Nick.'

It was more than strange; it was devastating. A lump the size of a golf ball rose into his throat. He swallowed, frantically.

'You know what?' Sal bunched a fist and punched him companionably on the arm. 'You ought to get yourself transferred to our place. You'd like it there. Honest!' Over her shoulder, as she ran to catch up with the others, she shouted: 'It's far more civilized!'

MacMaster had had to do without his sketches – the Judge Shoot, the Flasher on the Rocks, the Pet Jelly – Christopher's monologue, Nick's accompaniments. They were all there, on Nick's tape machine, and he supposed not even Gerald would deny him access if he actually went round and demanded it, but his feet wouldn't carry him along the road to Marden. One day they might; one day for old times' sake he might go back and gaze upon it; but he was not ready for it yet. MacMaster, caring only for his revue and not for anybody's possible sensibilities, urged him to try and remember what he had written.

'The show must go on, and all that ... I'm sure it's what Nick would have wanted.'

He probably could have remembered, had he set his mind to it; but when he tried, in his bedroom that same evening, he started weeping. He hadn't cried since he was a tiny kid. He was terrified lest Louise should come up and catch him at it. She would want to enfold him and comfort him and stroke his hair. She would want him to talk to her so that she could make soothing noises and say that she understood.

She didn't understand. How could she? Nobody did. They all thought that they did – but they were wrong. All of them!

'Nick, you bastard!' He sobbed it into his pillow, the crumpled reconstruction of the Judge Shoot clenched in his hand. 'You stupid dumb bastard . . . how could you?'

He told MacMaster next morning that he hadn't been able to come up with anything. 'It was all at the improvization stage, you know? We hadn't yet got anything down on paper.'

'So just give me the ideas – maybe you and I could work on them together.'

'I couldn't work on them with anyone else.' They had been his ideas and Nick's. He wasn't handing them over to MacMaster.

'If I may say so –' MacMaster wagged an admonitory finger within centimetres of Christopher's nose – 'this is hardly a very professional attitude. If ever there were a case when personal feelings should be set to one side –'

The finger waved, in front of his nose. Christopher was filled with a sudden intense loathing for the man. If it hadn't been for him and his damned revue Nick would still be here. He brought up his hand and chopped, angrily, at the intrusive finger.

'Stuff it!' he said.

Next morning he received one of his summonses to the Presence. He thought that probably MacMaster had gone whingeing, complaining of language and physical assault. He went expecting a bollocking, which would have bothered him not in the slightest: instead, he found Bogey wanting to talk about Nick, wanting to express sympathy and understanding for Christopher's plight, left on his own in a hostile environment. It very nearly cracked him up.

'So how are you coping?' Bogey leaned forward, solicitously, elbows on the desk, intently gazing at Christopher over the steeple of his fingers. 'I know you boys find it extraordinarily difficult to confide in people. I dare say I did when I was your age – for I was your age once, you know . . . in times gone by.'

Christopher attempted a dutiful smile: it wasn't often that Bogey attempted a pleasantry.

'I am aware that you have not always found school very easy to handle. I had hoped, recently – but then all this tragic business –' He paused. 'There is no likelihood, I fear, of Nicholas returning to Astley. His father spoke of a year's break, followed by private tuition. I believe he felt – possibly correctly – that a complete change of scene would be beneficial. I confess I have been wondering whether the same might not also apply to you. I feel you are not happy here with us at Astley. I feel you have not been happy for a long while. You may tell me if I am mistaken –'

Christopher remained silent.

'The climate, perhaps, is not right. There are those who fit, and those who do not. It should not be taken as a reflection on either the school or the individual: simply, they are not suited. You understand, I hope, that I am not asking you to leave? I would never do that. The decision is entirely yours. But I have wondered, perhaps, whether a less conventional environment . . . Calder High, I understand, has an excellent academic record. I would not normally advocate disrupting a pupil in his

A-level year, but I do feel, in your case, that possibly the benefits may outweigh the disadvantages. However, I have no wish to put pressure on you. What I would like you to do is go away and think about it, speak with your p – with your mother; speak, if you can, with someone who goes to the school. If you decide in favour of a change, then I am sure, in the circumstances, I would have no difficulty in arranging it. If, on the other hand, you opt to stay here with us –'

Then they would just have to put up with him.

'– we shall of course,' said Bogey, 'be delighted.'

A few days before Christmas he had a card from Nick. It said, simply, *Chris, Meilleurs voeux, Nick.* It was strange and disturbing to see Nick's handwriting, looking just the same as it had always looked. He couldn't make out the postmark on the envelope but the stamp was French. He wondered if they had gone back to Mont de Luciole.

Later that day, fortified by a glass of cooking sherry, when Louise had gone to work, he rang Marden. There was no reply; neither then, nor later, though he tried several times more. On Christmas Eve, without fortification this time, he sat down and scrawled a note in a left-over Christmas card of his mother's, a hideous thing with a drawing of angels – *Life is an incurable disease: there is nothing one can do save live with it. In the meanwhile, where are you and what is happening?* NICHTS WISSEN UNERTRÄGLICH IST.

Nichts wissen unerträglich ist. Not to know *was* unbearable.

He spent Christmas alone with Louise. They had been invited to go with the Sandersons to Salisbury, but Louise had made an excuse and declined. Privately, to

203

Christopher, she confided that she would have felt 'out of it . . . like an intruder. After all, they were your gran's relatives, not mine. You didn't want to go did you?'

He reassured her. Christmas with Louise might lack excitement, but Christmas with Glenn would be purgatory. Also, he would surely be haunted by the memories of last year, when he and Sal had crept away by themselves and got sloshed. Everyone had thought it a great joke, him and Sal doing that. Even his grandmother had pulled his leg. When he and Nick had done it, the whole world had come crashing about their ears.

Nichts wissen unerträglich ist . . . he could bear things a lot better if only he knew.

13

In January, Christopher transferred to Calder High. The evening before term started he had a call from Sal: 'You did it!' she said. 'You took my advice!'

He didn't tell her that he hadn't had much choice in the matter. For all his sweet-talk, Bogey had made it pretty plain he wanted him out; but if Sal chose to believe it had been her doing, he had no objection.

'D'you want to meet up at the bus stop? Then I can show you where to go and everything.'

He accepted the offer gratefully. The numbness of his last days at Astley was beginning to wear off and the first twinges of apprehension had already set in. He knew that by getting-up time tomorrow his whole body would be a violent knot of panic.

'Don't worry,' said Sal. 'You'll like it at Calder High. You're not getting cold feet, are you? You know what they say . . . the coward dies a thousand deaths, the hero dies but one?'

Which was all very well if you were a hero: he was not. He said, 'You know what they also say . . . better the devil you know –'

'Ah, crud! Nowhere could be as bad as that stuck-up

snob place. Just imagine – you won't have to put up with Glenn any more. That's got to be worth something! See you at eight-fifteen, don't be late.'

Sal was popular at Calder High; she was the sort of girl who would probably always be popular. It stood him in good stead, being, as it were, associated with her. All these new people he was with didn't realize he was mad and anti-social. They talked to him as if he were one of them, and after a bit, as he grew used to the sensation, he began tentatively to respond. Sometimes, rather more tentatively, he even initiated. As the weeks passed he found that he was actually able to sustain whole conversations. Nobody stared at him if he asked them a question; nobody, as far as he knew, whispered about him or sniggered. By half-term they still hadn't twigged that he was a nutter. He began, cautiously, to explore the idea that he might be more normal than he had thought.

Someone in his German group was having a half-term party. He hadn't got a girl to take – he hadn't quite progressed that far, though none of the myriad females whom he daily encountered in the corridors and classrooms had shown any signs of actually fleeing from him in horror – but he went along anyway. Robert, the boy whose party it was, had made a special point of asking him: 'There's someone who wants to meet you.'

The someone who wanted to meet him turned out to be a girl from Sal's year. She was small and rather mousy and her name was Ashley. She was taking business studies and domestic science, and had, according to Robert, 'been agitating about you since the beginning of term.' He found it hard to rouse much enthusiasm for either business studies or domestic science, but he couldn't help being flattered at the notion of anyone, however mousy and insignificant, finding him worthy of agitation. Not that she was as mousy and insignificant as that; just that he was more accustomed to Sal and her rumbustious unsquashability.

He said to Robert, casually, not wishing to wound the feelings of one who had agitated over him, 'Is Sal coming?'

'Well, Duncan is, so I guess he'll bring her.'

Duncan was the thing with the pony-tail.

'All the girls go for him,' said Ashley. 'I don't think he's specially attractive, do you?'

Christopher didn't think he was attractive at all. He thought he was a creep. Ashley said yes, he *was* a creep: 'I don't know what Sal sees in him.'

Duncan turned up at nine-thirty with Miranda Forbes. Sal arrived ten minutes later, by herself.

'They've had a row,' said Ashley. 'I'm not surprised, the way he puts it about ... thinks he's only got to whistle and it's off with your knickers.'

Sal had already had that sort of trouble with John Newman; you'd have thought she'd have learnt by now. She saw Christopher across the room and waved at him but didn't come over. She spent the evening sitting on cushions on the floor with a group of other girls, and it wasn't until the party was breaking up, round about midnight, that he had a chance to talk to her.

'How are you getting home?'

'Same as I came,' she said. 'By bus.'

'What, on your own?'

She pulled a face. 'We single women have to shift for ourselves.'

'If you wait a few minutes I'll come with you.'

'Oh?' She raised an eyebrow. 'What about Ash?'

'Her dad told her to call a cab. We're just waiting for it now.'

'You mean you're not going with her?'

Should he? He considered the suggestion, and rejected it. 'She lives all the way out at Petts Wood,' he said.

'Ay me . . .' Sal heaved a dramatic sigh. 'The path of true love never did run smooth.'

As they left together five minutes later she said, 'Poor old Ash! She's had her eye on you for weeks.'

'Didn't you warn her?'

'About what?'

'About me being boring and self-absorbed and anti-social, and the most unnatural person you've ever met?'

'Oh!' She shoved at him. 'You're not going to forgive me for that, are you?'

'I might,' he said. 'It depends.'

'What on?'

'Whether you do anything to earn my forgiveness.'

'What do you want me to do? Go down on my knees? Lick your boot laces?'

'Haven't got any.'

'So what's the price I have to pay?'

'Come out with me?' he said.

'Come out where?'

He shrugged. 'Anywhere you like.'

'I get to choose?'

'You get to choose.'

She laughed. 'I'll think about it,' she said. 'I'm not sure yet whether I actually want to be forgiven.'

Next morning, on a sudden inspiration, he took out

208

his *Penguin Book of English Verse* and looked up the poem she had sent him, all those months ago, after the Midsummer Ball. It was a sonnet, in fact, by Michael Drayton:

> *Since there's no help, come let us kiss and part,*
> *Nay, I have done: you get no more of me,*
> *And I am glad, yea glad with all my heart,*
> *That thus so cleanly, I myself can free.*
>
> *Shake hands for ever, cancel all our vows,*
> *And when we meet at any time again,*
> *Be it not seen in either of our brows,*
> *That we one jot of former love retain.*

That was as much as Sal had quoted. The last six lines had not, at the time, suited her purpose:

> *Now at the last gasp, of love's latest breath,*
> *When his pulse failing, passion speechless lies,*
> *When faith is kneeling by his bed of death,*
> *And innocence is closing up his eyes,*
> *Now if thou would'st, when all have given him*
>   *o'er,*
> *From death to life, thou might'st him yet recover.*

They might not have suited Sal's purpose, but they admirably suited his. He took a sheet of paper, wrote out the poem in its entirety in his best and most legible handwriting, underscored the last two lines in red pen and put it in an envelope. On the envelope he wrote: SAL. PERSONAL. BY HAND.

It was a long time since he had been to the house in Hawthorn Avenue. He approached it carefully, not wanting to be seen. If there were anyone in the front garden . . .

There wasn't. He stuffed the envelope through the letter box, turned and ran.

Later that evening, when he was watching television with Louise, the telephone rang. It was Sal.

'I've decided,' she said. 'We'll go to a disco . . .'

He went to a disco, he went to another disco. He went to a pop concert, he went to the cinema. He went to a party, where Ashley eyed him wistfully and was on her own, and he felt for her, because he knew what it was like, but he was with Sal and suddenly life was not such an incurable disease after all, he even began to think it might have something going for it – might even be worth the trouble of living right to the end. *Croyez-vous que la vie vaille la peine d'être vécue jusqu'à la fin?*

It had been Nick, originally, who had posed the question. They had discussed it up in the attic at Marden, one Saturday evening, tossing the arguments to and fro. Nick had maintained that the longer you lived the more likely you were to reach the conclusion that enough was enough: Christopher had agreed that possibly, by the time you reached old age – sixty, say, or seventy –

'Why wait till then?' Nick had said.

They had been just sixteen at the time.

He thought of Nick as one Saturday afternoon towards the end of term he walked with Sal in Holt Wood.

'Let's go and look at Marden,' he said.

'Marden? What's Marden?'

'Nick's old place.'

'Oh! OK. If you like.'

They walked, hand in hand, along the road which he

had walked so often, on a Saturday evening, clasping his pile of records. He still missed his Saturday evenings. He couldn't go back to them; but he missed them.

'How is Nick?' said Sal.

'I don't know,' he said.

'You don't *know*?' She stared at him. 'Don't you write?'

'I did write; once. He never replied.' Maybe that was because he'd never had the letter. Maybe they weren't sending things on to him.

'How come you only wrote once?' said Sal.

'They didn't want me to write at all.' He could admit it to her now. 'They reckoned I was a bad influence.'

She swung his hand, pondering this. 'I should have said, if anything, he was the one that was the influence.'

'Whichever. They wrote this note saying we weren't to communicate any more.'

'They did *what*?' She stopped, abruptly, in the middle of the pavement. 'That's *terrible*! They can't do things like that! You're not kids. How can they stop you from writing?'

'They can't stop me from writing, but they can stop him from getting my letters. Look, there's Marden. It's been sold.' Louise had relayed the information. 'Some stockbroker guy lives there now. Gerald and his dad have a flat up in town.'

'So where's Nick?'

He shook his head.

'You don't even know where he *is*? This is like something out of Victorian melodrama! You can't just cut people off like that.'

You could – they had. He stood, gazing up the tree-lined drive which led to Marden. It didn't hurt now as it had last term, but he would have liked at least to know that Nick was OK.

'I guess you must miss him pretty badly,' said Sal.

'I did, at first.'

'Not now?'

'Sometimes. Sometimes I do.' He thought that perhaps there was one part of him that always would. That even when he was ancient he would have moments of recalling. When he played a piece of music – *Nimrod*, say, or Mahler's Second – then, surely, he would remember. How could he not? Music and Nick were inextricably linked. For all that, the aching chasm which had been there inside him was gradually closing, would very soon be sealed. What, if anything, was contained within it – whether it held memories, or whether it remained a void – he was not sure; but he knew, now, that he could survive without Nick.

Sal was looking at him, seemingly waiting for something more.

'I can't explain,' he said. 'It's like – like the me that used to know Nick was another me, from another age; and the me that knows you grew out of that other me and has left it behind. So although I can't help thinking about him, and wondering about him, there isn't any way that *this* me could ever go back to being *that* me . . . if you see what I mean?'

'You mean if Nick ever came back you couldn't just pick up the threads?'

'No.' That was what worried him. Suppose Nick ever did come back and expected him to do just that?

'I guess it's difficult,' said Sal, 'when you've had a relationship that's been exclusive . . . I'm sorry I got mad at you that time. That time I called you all those things. I was stupid. I never realized – I mean, I thought

212

I could just come barging in and take over. I know now that you can't do that to people. I was pretty insulting, wasn't I? I didn't mean to be.'

'I expect I deserved it,' he said.

'You deserved *some* of it. Not all of it. All that stuff about knee pads, and that ... I guess I was just jealous. But I shouldn't have tried to come between you.'

'I never saw it that way.'

'You mightn't have done, but I bet Nick did.'

He frowned.

'Think about it! He'd just lost his grandmother, right? Now it must have seemed he was losing you, as well. The only two people he ever really cared about – the only two who actually meant anything to him. Doesn't that make sense?'

Christopher was silent.

'Well, doesn't it?' He shrugged. 'You're not convinced! Why not?'

'I suppose, basically, because ... because I'm not actually certain –'

'About what?'

He took a breath. 'I'm not actually certain that I did mean anything to him.'

It was Sal's turn to frown. 'Come on!' she said. 'After all those years?'

After all those years; he saw it now, with sudden clarity: it had never really been possible, getting through to Nick.

'It was like he'd put up some kind of – of barrier.'

Guy had been the Nick who lived behind that barrier: Oliver had been Christopher getting through the barrier. But Christopher as Christopher had never got through to Nick as Nick. He had always strongly

213

denied it when Louise complained of Nick's remoteness; but she had been quite right.

'He was a terribly unhappy sort of person,' said Sal. 'I realized that when I met him that time ... I never told you, did I, what happened?'

He looked at her. 'Did anything happen?'

'Well – no.' She gave a little laugh; it sounded slightly nervous. 'That was the point ... nothing did.'

There was a pause. He waited.

'I don't know why I'm telling you this,' said Sal. 'You'll only get mad at me.'

'I won't. I promise.' He had a sudden suspicion what she was going to say. He squeezed her hand. 'Go on! Tell me.'

'Well, we all got a bit ... a bit smashed. I mean, all of us except Nick. I know I swore I never would again – and I swear to you now that I never *will* again, *never* – but Gerald was there and he said why didn't we all go down the beach, and so we took these bottles with us, and it was fantastic, it was dark, and it was so warm, it was about midnight, and – oh! I don't know. It just sort of – happened. Except that nothing actually *did* happen; not with me and Nick.'

'You mean, it did for the others?' That toe-rag. That hypocrite. Going round seducing sixteen-year-old schoolgirls –

'Tanya said it did. I don't know; she's a bit of a fantasist. She had this thing about Gerald. That's why Nick and I –' She waved a hand. 'Anyway. Like I said. Nothing happened.'

'You mean –'

'I mean, *nothing happened*. Don't ask me why! I guess –' Sal forked, frantically, at her fringe – 'I guess he just didn't fancy me enough. But he did try! He really did *try*!'

Christopher winced.

'I'm not saying he was gay!'

'He wasn't,' said Christopher.

'Just that he seemed to have these problems, like . . . emotionally. You know?'

He nodded.

'It's like you said . . . about the barrier.'

Nick had said it better: *Tendrils reach into the void, and the green shoots wither for lack of nourishment.* The text books, less poetically, referred to it as alienation: the state of not being involved. He had once thought he might suffer from it himself. He knew now, thanks to Sal, that he didn't. He also knew the bottomless depths of terror it could plunge you to.

'Chris –' Sal slipped her hand back into his. 'You're not mad at me, are you?'

'I'm not mad at you.'

'I wouldn't want you to think I tried it on with Nick just to sort of – get even with you or anything.'

Such a thought would not have crossed his mind. Sal might be many things, but one thing she was not and that was mean of spirit.

They walked back, down the hill, hands linked in the sunshine.

'Isn't there any way at all you could get in touch with him?' said Sal. 'There surely must be some way?'

He supposed he could try another letter – it might just get through. But maybe Nick himself had wished to sever all connexions? Maybe, like Christopher, he was beginning at last to awake from his long hibernation.

'He knows where I am,' he said. 'If he wants to get in touch he knows how to do it.'

14

One Saturday evening towards the end of term, as Christopher was having a bath, loudly singing the Grand March from *Aida* as he soaped and scrubbed himself – he was going out with Sal later on, to a party somewhere in Chislehurst – the telephone rang. He could just hear it above the noise of sploshing bath water and the trumpetlike braying of his own voice. Seconds later Louise knocked at the door. (She would never come in, not when he was in the bath; it would have embarrassed both of them.)

'Christopher! It's for you.'

'OK.' Probably Sal telling him that she had managed to scrounge a lift for them. He draped a towel round himself, padded barefoot across the bathroom floor, opened the door and almost fell over Louise.

'It's someone called Guy,' she said.

Stupidly he said: 'Guy?'

'That's what he said . . .' Her voice trailed off. She looked at him nervously. 'Do you know anyone called Guy?'

'Oh! *Guy*. Yes. Of course . . . it's someone from school.'

'I thought, just for a moment –'

'It's all right.' He shepherded her down the stairs ahead of him, guiding her back into the sitting-room. 'You stay there. I'll get you a cup of tea when I've finished.'

He closed the door, padded back across the hall to the telephone, picked up the receiver. 'Guy?'

From the other end of the line, Nick's voice said, 'I wasn't sure she'd let you talk to me.'

'I don't know why you should have thought that. The prohibitions –' he turned his back on the sitting-room, hunching himself over the telephone – 'have all been on your side, not mine.'

'Yes, I know; I'm sorry. There wasn't any way I could get round it.'

He wondered about that. He found it hard to imagine Nick, succumbing to authority.

'So where are you?' he said. 'Where are you speaking from?'

'Call box. A couple of miles away.'

'Where?'

'Bottom of the hill.'

'*Here?* What are you –'

'I'll tell you when I see you. Come and meet me.'

'Ni–' He was just about to say 'Nick': he swallowed it just in time. He wouldn't put it past Louise to have her ear glued to the crack. She had obviously had her suspicions. 'I can't! I've got to go out.' He was due round at Sal's at eight o'clock. 'Why didn't you write?'

'Because I couldn't. I didn't know – I only decided at the last minute. Listen, I've come all this way –'

'Not just to see me!'

'Yes; in fact.'

Christopher pressed himself against the banisters,

one arm hooked round the newel post. 'You should have telephoned.'

'I am telephoning.'

'No! I mean – earlier.'

'It wasn't possible earlier, and anyway, what difference would it have made? If you're going out?'

'Well, I could have – could have arranged another time, or –'

'So arrange one!'

He thought, you can't do this to me. Not any more. You can't just turn up out of the blue and start dictating.

'N–' Once again, he stopped himself. 'I can't now! It's too late.'

'It's never too late.'

'Well, this time it is! You should have told me! I can't just –'

'Chris, I need to see you – just for half an hour, that's all. That's all I'm asking. Just half an hour!'

He had never known Nick ask for anything before. It wasn't Nick's style. Other people did the asking: Nick didn't need.

'Chris,' he said, 'please . . . I know I said it's never too late, but –'

The sitting-room door had opened and Louise had appeared. She mouthed apologetically at Christopher, pointing to the kitchen, making tea-pouring motions. He nodded.

'*Attends,*' he said, into the telephone. '*Il y a quelqu'un qui écoute.*'

'Well, while they're écouting why don't I make a suggestion? Why don't I come round to your place?'

'You're joking!' Nick come round here? Louise wouldn't give them five minutes on their own, never mind half an hour.

'I don't mean right to the door. Just the end of the road. Why don't I meet you there in . . . ten minutes?'

Still he hesitated.

'I'll see you on the corner, by the telephone box?'

'OK.' Louise disappeared into the kitchen. 'But I can only manage half an hour.'

'*Oui, mon capitaine! Ça c'est bien entendu!*'

It was only when he had put the receiver down that it occurred to him: how did Nick think he was going to get all the way from the bottom of Holt Hill to Dalmally Road in ten minutes? It couldn't be done; not unless he intended to run flat out.

He went back upstairs to get dressed, wondering how he was going to telephone Sal without Louise overhearing. He knew that he wasn't; not without sounding furtive. As he returned to the hall, wearing sweatshirt and jeans, with his jacket hanging by the loop from one finger, Louise emerged from the kitchen carrying two mugs of tea.

'I thought I'd make some,' she said. 'Do you want anything with it?'

'No, thanks. I'll be going out in a minute.'

'I thought you weren't going out till eight o'clock?'

'Had a change of plan.'

'Oh. Well –' She stood, holding the mugs. 'You've got time to drink your tea?'

'Yeah. Take it in there, I'll come and join you.'

He held the door for her, firmly shutting it once again behind her. He didn't know why he should want to keep from her the fact that Nick was in Holt Wood and that he was going to see him just for half an hour. It was something he felt instinctively it would be better for her not to know.

He took up the receiver and dialled Sal's number.

'Lo?' It was Glenn, monosyllabic as ever, who answered.

'Glenn, hi, this is Chris. Can I speak to Sal, please?'

'Oh. Right. Hang on.'

Sal was at the phone within seconds. 'What's happening?'

'Nothing's happening. It's just –' he lowered his voice – 'something's turned up. I'll tell you about it later. I might not be able to make it round your place till about eight-thirty. Is that OK?'

'Eight-thirty is *fine*. It'll give me a chance to do something about my hair ... I just tried curling it, I look like a clone of Shirley Temple. It's grotesque. You can make it as late as nine if you like.'

'Say about quarter-to?'

'OK. – Hey! It's nothing bad, is it?'

'What?'

'The thing that's turned up.'

'Oh. No. Just – unexpected. I'll tell you about it.'

'In *detail*.'

'In detail.'

'You'd better!'

'I will. I promise.'

There was a red Porsche parked at the corner of Dalmally and Ridgemount. He didn't think anything of it, was about to walk past, when the passenger door was flung open and a voice said, 'Hop in!'

'Nick?' He stooped, peering inside just to make sure. 'What are you doing with a car?'

'It's not mine, it's beloved brother's ... I nicked it. Get in, we'll go for a spin.'

'Don't forget, I c–'

'I know! You've only got half an hour. Where are you going? Saturday night binge?'

'Going to a party.' He wrestled for a moment with conscience, then: 'You could come along if you wanted.'

'Me? At a party? You know I don't fit in. I've given up trying. You can only bash your head against a brick wall for so long; after that you lose consciousness. Anyway, I'd only cramp your style. Who are you going with? Anyone I know?'

Concentrating on the intricacies of fastening his seat belt, he mumbled: 'Sal.'

'Oh, yes! I remember. The one from Down Under. You always had a thing about her.'

The Porsche plunged forward, out on to the main Bromley Road. Christopher said, 'I didn't have a thing about her, we just happened to meet up again. After you – left –'

'You mean, after I was forcibly abducted.'

Sidetracked, he said: 'Were you?'

'As good as.'

'Why didn't you ever write to me?'

'Didn't feel like writing.'

'Did you get my note?'

'Yes, I got it.'

'So w–'

'You were going to tell me what happened. After I was abducted.'

'Oh. Yes. Well, I – um – I transferred to Calder High. Bogey seemed to think that as you were having a change of scene I ought to have one, too. He wasn't actually asking me to leave, you understand –'

'Just politely chucking you out. Still, it seems to have had happy results.'

'Yeah. Well –'

'It's all right.' Nick sounded amused. 'You don't

have to apologise. I didn't expect you to remain celibate on my account.' He leaned forward and pressed a button somewhere on the dashboard. 'Let's have some music.'

The opening bars of the *Enigma Variations* came singing into the car. Gerald's car.

'Doesn't he mind you borrowing his Porsche?' said Christopher.

'Doesn't know I've got it.'

'Oh?'

'I told you, I nicked it.'

'How?'

'Easy. I got a cab from Heathrow, went to the flat and helped myself.'

'So what's he going to do when he finds out?'

'Who knows? Who cares? He's over in the States for a month. By the time he gets back –' Nick humped a shoulder. The car went bellying out across the centre line, causing an oncoming vehicle to swerve sharply and lean on the horn. 'Tosspot!' said Nick.

Nervously, Christopher said, 'You'd better make sure you don't go and mark it.'

'Why? It's only a bit of machinery.'

'It may only –' involuntarily, he shoved both hands against the dashboard as the Porsche took a corner on two wheels – 'it may only be a bit of machinery but I'll bet it cost a small fortune!'

'So it's insured. He can get another. He's loaded.'

'What kind of philosophy's that supposed to be?'

'Ah, stop whingeing! Enjoy yourself!'

Christopher wiped a hand across his brow: he was not surprised to find it wet. 'Where are we headed, anyway?'

'Nowhere in particular. Just out for a spin. Why? Where did you feel like going?'

222

He was beginning to think that he didn't feel like going anywhere. 'I never knew you could drive,' he said.

'Anyone can drive. Morons can drive. There isn't anything to it. See that?' Nick pressed his foot down. The needle on the speedo zipped up fast to 130. 'That's the gas pedal. There's another one somewhere called the brake. And once you've mastered that, that's it. *Un morceau de gâteau*, as they say en franglais.'

Christopher swallowed. 'You don't think –' he strove to keep his voice calm and unhysterical – 'you don't think we need a touch of brake right now, do you?'

'Not really. We're on a motorway. Why? Are you bottling? I hope you're not going to make a mess of my brother's Porsche.'

'What's it matter?' Feebly, he attempted a come-back. 'He's insured.'

'Not against people who shit themselves.'

'If you'd told me what you were planning I'd have worn my incontinence pad.'

Nick grinned. The needle gradually fell back, down past the 100 mark. Ninety . . . eighty . . . seventy.

'That do you, granddad?'

'It's just . . . I do have this appointment to keep. And I bet you don't have a UK driving licence!'

'Don't have any driving licence.'

'Jesus, Nick! Are you crazy?'

'Out of my mind! I thought you knew that? Why else do you suppose I was smuggled out of the country beneath a blanket with my alcoholic mother to keep an eye on me?'

'H–how is your mother?'

'How is she? At this moment in time? Pissed to the eyeballs, I should imagine.'

'Did she come over with you?'

'No, I escaped. While she was off sozzling.'

'You mean she doesn't know you're here?'

'Probably not.'

Christopher was silent. He sat, staring ahead at the long line of lights on the motorway, thinking of Sal, thinking of the party they had to go to in Chislehurst. He wondered where they were. He didn't even know which motorway they were on. It could be the M25. You heard bad things about the M25. Fog, tailbacks, multiple pile-ups . . . He turned to look at Nick. He supposed, even if he didn't have a licence, it didn't mean he wasn't a perfectly competent driver. Nick was usually competent at the things he did. Still, he would have been happier if they could just have sat in a pub and talked.

'So what are your – ah – plans?' he said.

'Long-term? Haven't got any.'

'Bogey said something about – a year's break then – private tuition.'

'Wishful thinking.'

'Will you be coming back over here?'

'What do you mean, coming back? I am back!'

'No, I mean . . . permanently.'

'I am back permanently. Inasmuch,' said Nick, 'as I only bought a one-way ticket.'

'So what are you going to do? Live up in town, in the flat?'

Nick was silent.

'You must have some idea! I mean, what suddenly . . . brought you over here?'

'I told you, I came to see you; also to take a last look at the house. I was going to ask if I could go in, but then I had second thoughts . . . if poor old Tipsy

Anna rang up they might go and spill the beans.'

He was about, foolishly, to say 'Who's Tipsy Anna?' His brain seemed to have seized up, but he wasn't used to Nick openly alluding to his mother's alcohol problem.

'Is she – any better?' he said.

'About as better as I am. We're not exactly the ideal combination.'

There was a silence. The car roared on, along the motorway. Dimly, Christopher noticed a sign saying Sevenoaks.

'They wouldn't let me come and visit you,' he said. 'I tried to, but they wouldn't let me.'

'That's right, I was guarded day and night for fear of you getting at me.'

'You're not serious?'

'No: I'm not serious ... it was more for fear of me getting at me.'

'But you're OK now?' said Christopher.

'Was I ever OK? I've always been a nutcase. Haven't I? All the time you've known me ... would you have said I was well-adjusted?'

'I never really thought about it.'

'Liar!'

'I used to think about whether *I* was well-adjusted.'

'You might have been, if you hadn't met me.'

'No. That's just a cop-out.'

Nick smiled. 'You can't talk to me about cop-outs ... mine was the biggest cop-out of the lot. Or at least, it would have been.'

'But you never *seriously* –'

'Seriously?' said Nick.

'I mean –' They always said that an attempt at suicide was a cry for help. But how could you put that to someone who'd actually been through it? How, without sounding incredibly patronizing?'

'If you mean what I think you mean, then the answer is yes. I did. Seriously. But I bungled it. I don't usually bungle things, do I? You wouldn't say that I was by nature a bungler?'

'No,' said Christopher. He said it loudly and positively. 'I wouldn't. That's why I reckoned it must have been more in the nature of a – a symbolic gesture. Because if you'd really wanted to do it, then you'd have done it. Not like me. I could screw up on anything.'

'But you think I'm more efficient.'

'I know you are,' said Christopher.

'So what are you saying? My conscious and my sub-conscious were at war, and my sub-conscious won?'

'Something like that.'

'Well, it's an interesting theory; I'll bear it in mind.'

Surreptitiously, Christopher glanced at his watch. 'We ought to be turning back pretty soon,' he said.

'In a minute. I haven't told you why I wanted to see you. I thought of writing, but we always used to wait until we could actually get together . . . I had this thought,' said Nick, 'about Guy and Oliver.'

Christopher felt his heart plummet. Guy and Oliver were gone; part of a past which was dead and buried. No way, now, could they be resurrected.

Carelessly he said: 'I haven't been thinking about them too much just lately.'

'Me neither,' said Nick. 'Not until just a few days ago. And then it came to me, and I knew I had to come over and tell you. You see, what I thought –'

He desperately didn't want to hear what Nick had thought.

226

'– I thought that Guy and Oliver would have made this pact. They –'

'I don't want to know!' said Christopher. He leaned forward and turned up the volume switch on the tape deck. A swell of sound filled the car. So wrought-up was he that he didn't immediately recognize it.

'*Nimrod*,' said Nick. 'And it's no good saying you don't want to know. Whether you want to know or whether you don't want to know is quite irrelevant: I've already thought it.'

And once a thought had been developed, it stood for all time. That was one of the rules of the game. Except that it had ceased, long ago, to be anything like a game.

The great arcs of *Nimrod* surged about the car. Nick's voice talked on, talking through it, talking over it. The needle on the speedo rose, and went on rising.

'For Christ's sake!' said Christopher. 'Let's get off this bloody motorway!'

'You want to get off the motorway? We'll get off the motorway!'

There was an exit coming up about a hundred yards ahead of them. The car slewed towards it, cutting a swathe across the two inner lanes.

'Jesus Christ!' screamed Christopher. Instinctively, he threw his hands to his head. Somewhere behind them, all hell broke loose.

'What's the matter? You bottling again?' Nick laughed, reached forward and turned the volume on the tape even higher.

The sound of Nick laughing above the thundering roar of Elgar was the last thing that Christopher remembered.

*

They said afterwards, when he was lying immobile in a hospital bed, with his leg suspended in a complicated mess of wires and pulleys, his body wrapped up like an Egyptian mummy, they said that he was lucky to be there.

'You're a very lucky young man,' they said. 'A *very* lucky young man.'

They kept nagging at him, badgering him, asking him, 'What happened?' They wanted to know, had Nick been drunk? Had he been on drugs? Had there been a fight, an argument, some kind of stressful situation? They had no problems with him crashing the car into a tree. Young man, no licence, stolen vehicle, going too fast: that was all right, they could cope with that. It was, as one of the interviewing officers drily said, an everyday occurrence: 'Bloody young fools going joyriding, putting everyone else at risk.'

But to do what he had done on the motorway – that really bugged them. That defied all comprehension. Flew in the face of all experience. Even bloody young fools going joyriding didn't do what Nick had done.

'No one in their right mind –'

They left the suggestion hanging, waiting for him to bite. *Had* Nick been in his right mind? He remained stubbornly silent. Nick himself had gone beyond reach of their probing. His life had been tormented while he lived it; he thought, now, that they might let him alone.

'You are co-operating,' Louise said, 'aren't you? I think it's the least you can do, considering. It's a miracle no one was killed.'

When she said no one, she wasn't counting Nick. Nick was the perpetrator: the bloody young fool putting other people's lives at risk. As if he had done it maliciously. As if he could be held responsible. She seemed to have forgotten that a few short months ago she had talked of what he must have suffered and no one bothering to notice.

'More money than sense,' she said. 'Your grand-mother was quite right, money isn't everything, not by a long chalk. And *why* you had to go with him, I shall never know!'

'I went,' he said, 'because he asked me.'

'So you have to do whatever he asks you?'

She didn't understand, and he knew that it was useless trying to explain. How could she or anyone, except, possibly, Sal, appreciate the significance of Nick, of all people, admitting to a need? Even if they could, it would seem too gross a betrayal of friendship to tell it to the world.

'Getting into the car with him! You must have known he didn't have a licence. But it was always the way, wasn't it? He called the tune, you danced to his bidding. I used to think, if that boy told you to put a noose round your neck and jump from the nearest tree you'd do it.'

He made no attempt to defend himself. It was, he thought, his final act of loyalty towards Nick.

Sal came to see him, and defiant of hospital rules sat perched on the side of the bed. 'At least,' she said, 'they can't get at him. I know it's not much solace, but –'

'It was what he wanted.' And therefore was a solace; of sorts. Nick wouldn't have thanked anyone for drag-ging him from the wreckage alive. In the battle between his conscious and his sub-conscious, his conscious, on this occasion, had won.

'I suppose it would be too terribly corny to say that now he's at peace?' Sal grew slightly pink as she said it. It was the sort of thing you couldn't really say without growing slightly pink.

'Just because a thing's corny,' said Christopher, 'doesn't mean to say it doesn't help.'

'Does it help?'

He nodded. He still found there were moments when he couldn't trust himself to speak.

'OK.' She bunched her fist and brought it down gently on his hand, lying outside the bed covers. 'I'll do the talking. You just grunt . . . one for yes, two for no . . . Nick's mum asked me to ask you something. She wanted to come here. Did your mum tell you?' He shook his head. 'She wanted to come and see you but your mum said she'd rather she didn't . . . *if* she didn't mind.' He rolled his eyes. 'Yeah, I know,' said Sal, 'people oughtn't to make these sort of decisions for other people, but your mum's had a really rough time of it. That night, when you didn't get back . . . I think she knew something had happened. Even before the police arrived. She just knew. 'Cause when I rang her up to see where you were, I said you'd told me you might be a bit late, except that was hours ago, and she said you'd gone off with someone called Guy, and then she said, "But I think it's Nick." And she just had this feeling something bad had happened. You know? So then I went round there, and the police came, and they brought us to the hospital and everything, and while we were here, waiting for you to come out of the operating theatre, Nick's mum arrived, and it was awful 'cause she was all crying and your mum accused her of being drunk, and actually I think she probably had been drinking, on the plane or somewhere, but she wasn't actually *drunk*, she was just in a state . . . it seems she'd discovered Nick had gone and she'd rung his brother and no one was there, so she'd just jumped on the first flight over. She said the police were already at the flat when she got there — I guess they'd identified the car, or something. She didn't even *know* about the car . . . anyway, soon as your mum went off to see you, she came and sat with me. She said when I got to visit you and it was OK for you to talk would I ask you something, and I said I would, and —'

Sal took a breath.

'What it is, what she wants me to ask you is, whether . . . whether Nick did it deliberately? I know you said it was what he wanted, but —'

He thought of Nick as he had last seen him, behind the wheel of the Porsche, exultantly laughing as the strains of *Nimrod* filled the car. *If ever there were music for dying to . . .*

'He didn't do it deliberately,' said Christopher. 'He did it because he couldn't help it. He tried the best he could — he tried to be one of us.' He'd come to the party: he just hadn't been able to fit in. But you couldn't say it was his fault — you couldn't say he'd done it deliberately. 'Like if someone has a coronary . . . they can't help what they do. If the car goes out of control, or something, you don't say that it was their fault. You don't hold them to blame. They don't cause accidents on purpose. Well, neither did Nick! Just because the one thing's physical, and the other —'

'OK,' said Sal. 'OK, take it easy. Don't get worked up or they'll come and throw me out. Just relax! You're not meant to be stimulated. I was given strict instructions . . . *whatever you do, don't get him excited.*'

'In that case —' he said it rather shakily — 'you'd better get off the bed.'

'Why? Is that getting you excited?'

'What do you think?'

'I wouldn't know,' said Sal. She lowered her eyes, mock demure. 'I don't know too much about this sort of thing.'

'You want me to tell you?'

'Not if it's anything crude.'

He was about to say, 'Let me put it this way . . . if I weren't all done up like a parcel –' He tried to say it, but the words wouldn't come. He turned his head into the pillow.

'Chris?' Sal bent over him, anxiously. 'What's the matter?'

'How can I – lie here –' His voice was muffled, hoarse with the tears which could not be shed – 'lie here and – joke, when it's – only – three days –'

Her cheek pressed against his. 'It was what he wanted.'

'Yes, but I – I think he wanted it – for both of us.'

'So he got half of what he wanted. That's a lot more than some people ever get. He couldn't expect to have it all . . . that would have been greedy.'

Little better than a murderer; that was the way Louise had put it. His friend Nick. His only friend. Lying dead on a mortuary slab. More alone than he had ever been. God, if there is a God, be merciful! *Dona eis requiem* . . .

When the time came for Sal to go, he quite desperately didn't want her to. So long as she was there, the nightmare could be held at bay: he knew that the minute she left it would start again. She was the only one who could even begin to understand.

'Don't worry,' she said. 'I'll be back. Now that they've let me in, there won't be any holding me! Listen, I'll be talking to Nick's mum tonight. I promised her I would, soon as I'd seen you. Do you want me to give her any message or anything?'

He shook his head. What could he possibly have to say to Susan Sheringham?

'Well, if you're sure.' She squeezed his hand. 'Just take care of yourself! I'll see you at the weekend.'

He lay watching as she moved off across the ward. Suddenly, as she reached the exit, he thought of something. He hoisted himself on one elbow. 'Sal!'

She turned.

'There is just one thing –'

'What's that?'

'When they – arrange things –'

'Yes?'

'Tell them to play *Nimrod* for him.'

'*Nimrod*?'

'From the *Enigma*.'

'*Nimrod* from the *Enigma*.'

'Yes. Tell them. It's very important.'

'OK.' She stuck up a thumb. 'I'll see to it.'

He lay back against the pillows. He knew that he could rely on Sal.